THE
BURIED
AND THE
DROWNED

A SHORT STORY COLLECTION

J.F. PENN

The Buried and the Drowned. A Short Story Collection.
Copyright © J.F. Penn (2025).
Individual stories first published 2012–2025.

Special Edition Hardback ISBN: 978-1-913321-41-3
Paperback ISBN: 978-1-913321-42-0
Large Print ISBN: 978-1-913321-43-7
Ebook ISBN: 978-1-913321-44-4
Audiobook ISBN: 978-1-917252-00-3

Requests to publish work from this book should be sent to: joanna@JFPenn.com

Cover and interior images generated by J.F. Penn on Midjourney with commercial license

Cover and Interior Design: JD Smith Design

www.CurlUpPress.com

CONTENTS

FOREWORD

We are all, in some way, either buried or drowned.

Buried by the weight of expectation, drowned in the relentless currents of world events. Buried by secrets, drowned in the depths of our own ambition. Buried by the past, drowned in the tides of history.

But there are other kinds of burial, other forms of drowning — the literal ones that preserve and transform, that hold secrets in the dark until someone is brave or foolish enough to disturb them. And sometimes, if we are lucky — or perhaps unlucky — we brush against the thin veil that separates our world from the things that have been buried, drowned — and perhaps still wait for us.

To be buried or to be drowned is to be overwhelmed, yet also preserved. Peat and sand, ice and water. They hold things in stasis, waiting for a storm or an archaeologist's trowel to bring them back to the light, and in these stories I invite you to join me in uncovering them.

These stories all have seeds in my history. Places that have left their mark, experiences I can't forget, and questions I still struggle to answer.

Some stories go back to childhood. After my parents' divorce, my dad used to take me and my brother to Bristol Zoo, a place of wonder that became a landscape of emotional memory.

When the zoo closed for redevelopment decades later, I found myself wondering what secrets might be unearthed from its Victorian foundations. That question spun itself into *Beneath the Zoo*, a tale of architecture, ambition, and the dark legacy of a father's work, exploring how the past is never truly buried and how its unearthing can force terrible choices.

Other stories stem from life changes that left their impact.

Back in 2000, burned out from my corporate life in London, I travelled to the other side of the world and scuba-dived at the Poor Knights Islands of New Zealand. Beneath the waves, I found a peace that the surface world could not offer, and I also felt the pull of the deep, a temptation to keep descending. That feeling, that 'call of the void,' resurfaces in *Between Two Breaths*, where I hope you can glimpse the possibility of ultimate escape.

These tales span more than a decade of my writing life. The earliest story in the collection, *Sins of Treachery*, was written over a decade ago, while the most recent, *The Black Church*, emerged from my fiftieth birthday trip to Iceland in early 2025, the year of this book's publication.

The real Black Church on the starkly beautiful Snæfellsnes peninsula inspired the story of a man grappling with a crisis of faith at the edge of the world, discovering that some things are buried for our protection. The raw power of that landscape, dominated by the Snæfellsjökull glacier, brought home the humbling reality of deep time, a theme that echoes through many of my stories and other works of fiction and memoir. That sense of place, of landscapes that hold ancient power and human secrets, is the thread that connects all these stories.

I've always been drawn to the darker corners of human experience, perhaps because they reveal the most truth about who we really are. In these liminal spaces, between land and sea, past and present, the sacred and the profane, we discover what we're truly capable of.

From hidden tombs beneath Paris, to the sacrificial shores of Norfolk, and the desperate choices made in the heat of a glass furnace or the lens of a war photographer's camera, these stories explore the threshold between our world and another, between science and myth, faith and oblivion. My characters stand at a precipice, faced with a choice:

to retreat to the safety of the known, or to take a breath and plunge into the abyss.

I invite you now to take that plunge. To dig a little deeper. To hold your breath and descend. To see what waits for you in the dark, in the quiet, in the deep — and to discover what rises when the buried and the drowned finally break free.

J.F. Penn, Bath, England
July 2025

THE
BLACK
CHURCH

DARKNESS CAME EARLY IN Iceland, swallowing the landscape by three in the afternoon. David Thornwell gripped the steering wheel of his rental SUV, his knuckles white as he navigated the final stretch of road toward Búðir out on the remote Snæfellsnes peninsula. The local weather service had promised a brief window between storm systems that should have given him enough time to reach his destination, but it seemed the gap was closing. He could feel the wind picking up, buffeting the vehicle with each gust that swept across the barren, snow-covered lava fields.

If the weather closed in, he might be stranded out here for days. There was still time to turn around, retreat to the warmth and comfort of Reykjavík, but what was there to truly go back for?

David took a deep breath and accelerated into the storm.

Soon after, he crested a rise, and a gust of wind opened the snow like a curtain, revealing the Black Church of Búðir, its tar-blackened walls a stark geometric slash against the pristine white of the landscape.

Behind it, shrouded in low-hanging clouds, the massive Snæfellsjökull glacier dominated the horizon. The glacier had come and gone with every ice age, each time smothering a seven-hundred-thousand-year-old volcano. A span of time incomprehensible to the human mind, and the kind of perspective David desperately sought here at the ends of the earth.

He pulled up next to the church and switched off the engine. He had come for a silent retreat, but there was no silence here. The storm howled and a bitter wind moaned across the Búðahraun lava field. As David stepped out of the vehicle, a blast slammed the car door shut behind him as if the wind wanted to trap him here, freezing his blood to ice.

The air tasted of snow and volcanic earth, clean and harsh, and salt from the bitter sea only a few hundred metres away. The cold burned David's lungs with each breath as he hurried to grab his gear from the back: a week's worth of food, a down sleeping bag rated for arctic conditions, lots of warm clothing, and a leather satchel containing his journal and well-worn Bible. He grabbed the bags and carefully picked his way through the snowdrifts to the entrance.

The walls of the church were painted with traditional ship's pitch to protect against the harsh elements, and the black absorbed what little light remained in the winter sky. White trim around the windows and door provided the only contrast. A simple bell tower crowned the structure, its cross barely visible against the darkening clouds.

Originally established in 1703, the church had fallen into disrepair, but was rebuilt in 1848 to serve the local community. The very act of building it here was testament to Icelandic fortitude, and a faith that stood proud amongst the frozen wilderness.

David approached the heavy wooden door, fishing the key from his pocket with numb fingers. The Anglican Church maintained a reciprocal relationship with various Lutheran parishes in Iceland, and when he had requested a winter silent retreat, they offered him this — a week alone in one of the most isolated churches in Europe.

If he couldn't hear God's voice out here — so close to nature, so far from the clamour of the city and the demands of his parish — perhaps there was no voice to hear at all.

As he put the key in the lock, David noticed strange gouge marks on either side of the door, scratches made by what looked like giant claws. Perhaps some local creature tried to get in and shelter from the violence of the winter storms, although he couldn't recall reading about anything with claws that big roaming the remote peninsula.

The lock clicked, and he hurried inside, shutting out the elements as he looked around at his temporary retreat.

The church interior was warmer than the brutal cold outside, though still far from comfortable. His breath came in visible puffs as he set down his supplies and reached for the light switch.

Electric bulbs flickered to life. White-painted walls rose to a peaked ceiling supported by dark wooden beams. A modest altar faced rows of wooden pews with enough seating for perhaps fifty people, though David suspected the congregation was rarely that large in this remote location. A small organ sat to one side, its keys yellowed with age.

The windows lacked curtains or other adornments, offering an unobstructed view of the snow-covered landscape that had remained essentially unchanged for five thousand years. During the brief hours of daylight, worshippers could see the glacier looming in the distance, a reminder of forces far greater than human concerns. Right now, God seemed just as distant and uncaring.

David set about arranging his temporary living space with the same methodical precision he brought to writing his sermons. He spread his sleeping bag over a camp bed near the altar, positioning it so he could see out the windows while he lay in the warm cocoon. He put his books on the front pew: commentaries on Job and Ecclesiastes, and a well-worn copy of C. S. Lewis's *A Grief Observed*.

At the bottom of his satchel, wrapped carefully in a teal silk scarf, was Emma's gold cross. It was the only jewellery she had ever worn, apart from her wedding ring. As he placed it onto his Bible by his pillow, the scent of antiseptic flooded back to him. Emma's fingers, bird-thin after months of treatment, clutched the tiny cross as the IV drip marked time in the corner. "We're not alone in this," she had whispered, her voice hoarse but certain. "You will never be alone, my love. He will be with you."

Even then, with her hair gone and her skin translucent as parchment, the lines of pain evident on her face, she thought only of her God and her husband. Her faith had been tactile, immediate, something she could hold on to when everything else was slipping away. If only he had the same fortitude.

Exploring the small church further, David found a modest collection of books and journals stacked behind the organ.

He thumbed through the top one. The earliest entries dated back decades, written in a mixture of Icelandic, English, and German by various caretakers and visitors who had spent winter months alone in the church. Notes about the quality of the silence, the shapes and colours of the aurora borealis, and the strange visions that came in the endless dark of the Icelandic winter. Some of the nightmares had claws, and David frowned, glancing back towards the door and its unusual markings.

Beneath the journals, he found two books he recognised: Jules Verne's *Journey to the Centre of the Earth* and *Under the Glacier* by Halldór Laxness. Both were set in this area and both grappled with the relationship between humanity and the vast timescale of geology. Verne's scientific optimism and Laxness's mystical scepticism provided different responses to the humbling reality of deep time that was so tangible in this place.

David looked out the window at the distant glacier; though almost invisible in the storm, its presence was still dominant. How insignificant we humans are on the face of the earth, he thought. Just a flicker of light against the dark expanse of history. Logically, this awareness should put his grief into perspective, and yet, the weight of it still pressed down upon him, crushing his faith to dust and ashes.

Emma's faith had only become stronger at the end, her frail fingers holding her simple cross as she spoke of God's plan with a certainty that David both envied and resented. He had prayed for her healing with all the theological sophistication his doctorate could muster. He marshalled every argument for divine intervention he had learned at seminary. But God remained silent, inactive, uncaring, while his beloved wife withered away in a hospital bed.

He was supposed to believe they would see each other again in Heaven, but he had never really accepted that. His faith was more procedural, intellectual, of a kind that offered no solace when all meaning bled out of his life.

But at least here, he could focus on the basics. Eat, sleep, read. Try to pray. Wait out the storm. He could make a choice each day to keep living, or walk out into the storm and lie down on the frozen earth, letting the snow cover him and his bones disintegrate into this ancient place.

For now, it was worth staying alive a little longer for the promise of a hot cup of tea and one of his freeze-dried camping meals. He rifled through his pack. Spaghetti bolognese and chocolate pudding. David smiled. It was enough.

He set up his tiny camping stove, enjoying the heat as it thawed his icy fingers. As the water boiled, the wind outside picked up, rattling the windows and sending snow spiralling past the glass in hypnotic patterns. As he'd guessed in the car, the storm had arrived earlier than predicted, and he might indeed be stranded here. But the thought didn't frighten him. If anything, it brought a sense of relief. It made life that much simpler.

After eating, he hunkered down in his sleeping bag, watching the storm through the windows. Sleep proved as elusive as it had been for many weeks now, so David lay awake, listening to the wind hammer snow against the walls of the church and the creak of the old timber as the building settled against the cold.

The storm blew over, the skies cleared, and the aurora borealis came in the small hours, spilling green light through the church windows. David sat up in his sleeping bag, his breath misting in the frigid air. The aurora danced across the sky in curtains of emerald and jade, pink and stark white, casting the snow-covered lava field in an otherworldly glow that made the landscape appear fluid, alive.

Despite the brutal temperature, David pulled on his boots and heavy coat, and pushed out into the night, steeling himself against the cold.

The aurora moved across the sky in slow, hypnotic waves, colours shifting from green to purple to a deep, electric blue that seemed to pulse with its own heartbeat. David stood shivering, utterly insignificant beneath the cosmic dance of charged particles and magnetic fields.

This was beauty on a scale that dwarfed human creations, older than scripture, older than faith itself. As he watched, a strange vertigo washed over him, as if he stood outside of time, a witness to the light of creation. The aurora had danced like this for millennia, before humans had words for God or grief or redemption. It had seen the rise and fall of empires, and even the great and powerful humbled by death.

The cold finally drove David back inside, but sleep remained elusive. He took one of the leather journals from the pile and settled back into his sleeping bag to read by the narrow beam of his head torch.

The entries were a mixture of practical observation and personal reflection, written in careful script by pastors and caretakers who had spent winter months in isolation.

Most were unremarkable — notes about supply deliveries, the condition of the building, brief theological meditations on the nature of solitude. But as David read deeper into one journal, the tone shifted.

Pastor Erik Magnusson had spent an entire winter here, and his entries grew increasingly strange as the months progressed.

The aurora came again last night, stronger than I have ever seen. The light seemed to pool in corners of the church, in places where it should not reach. My prayers have turned to protection. "When I sit in darkness, the Lord will be a light to me." Micah 7:8

David turned the page to another entry.

The old records speak of this place before the church was built. The stories are troubling. The settlers speak of things beneath the lava that should not be disturbed. Things that long for the age of humans to pass, that they might roam the land once more.

David frowned as he found a loose piece of paper tucked between the leaves of the journal.

If the aurora comes on consecutive nights, and the earth trembles, and the sea shows patterns that mirror the sky, ring the bell to send what arrives back to the depths beneath.

David looked up from the note to find that the green light of the aurora had penetrated the church interior, pooling in corners and casting shadows that moved independently of the light source. The hair on the back of his neck stood up as he watched tendrils of luminescence creep along the walls like living things, gathering in the spaces between the wooden beams.

There was no wind now, as if the earth held its breath to watch the celestial display. The silence was so profound that David could hear his own heartbeat, his own breathing, the soft rustle of paper in his hands. But beneath that, almost below the threshold of hearing, was something else. A low, rhythmic sound that might have been waves against the nearby shore — or something vast breathing in the depths of the earth below.

By morning, the wind had returned with renewed fury, driving snow against the windows in crystal-line sheets. David brewed coffee on his stove, the familiar ritual an anchor in this place that seemed increasingly unmoored from the ordinary world.

As he sat in the front pew, cradling the warm cup between his palms, David wrestled with a growing urge to pack his things and head back to Reykjavík.

He could drive to the capital, catch the next flight to London, submit his resignation to the bishop, and end his charade of a ministry that had become hollow since Emma's death. No one would blame him. Grief was acceptable grounds for stepping away from the pulpit.

But even as he considered the thought, another part of him rebelled against it. He had come here for answers, seeking some kind of encounter with the divine that might restore his shattered faith and give him a reason to continue. To leave now would be to admit that God was truly absent from this place — and his heart — and that the silence contained nothing but emptiness.

The theological implications alone troubled him. If God was omnipresent, as scripture taught, then He was here in this stark wilderness as surely as He was in the comfortable parish back home in Somerset. Perhaps even more so.

This landscape had been shaped by forces that operated on a timescale that dwarfed human history. Perhaps he needed to confront not the absence of God, but his own inability to perceive the divine, to see through petty human concerns to the wilder, ancient elements that stood so far above them.

David made his decision. He would stay.

This discomfort, this sense of spiritual vertigo, might be exactly what he needed to find a new perspective.

Around midday, David bundled himself in his heaviest clothes and ventured outside. The brief window of winter daylight revealed a landscape transformed. Snow had turned the tortured shapes of the ancient lava field into something sculptural, highlighting textures and patterns that spoke of unimaginable heat and violence eons ago.

David walked carefully across the uneven ground toward the distant sound of water lapping on the North Atlantic shore.

At the water's edge, the sea stretched away toward the horizon, dark and restless beneath the winter sky. There were strange patterns in the water, geometric shapes that caught the pale light and reflected it back in configurations that seemed too regular to be natural. Hexagonal forms that reminded him of photographs he had seen of basalt columns, but these moved and shifted with the rhythm of the waves.

For a moment, he forgot the cold entirely, mesmerised by the display. This was beauty of a different order than anything he had experienced in his tidy English parish — wild, alien, indifferent to human presence yet magnificent in its very indifference. If God was present here, He was not the gentle shepherd of pastoral theology, but something far more ancient and awe-inspiring. Something terrible.

The wind began to pick up again, driving ice crystals against his exposed face with stinging force. David retreated to the church, stamping snow from his boots and shedding his outer layers in the relative warmth of the interior.

The patterns in the water lingered in his mind, and he returned to the journals with renewed purpose. He paged through mundane details of parish life, records of births, deaths, marriages, struggles with bills and roof repairs that plagued every church he had ever known. Human lives begun and ended in this remote place, no different in their essential concerns from the congregation he had left behind in Somerset.

But beneath the familiar entries, he noticed other things. Notations that seemed distinctly un-Christian, references to old customs and beliefs that predated the church's construction. Runes sketched in margins, alongside Biblical verses of protection. Mentions of local families who still left offerings at certain stones during the winter solstice. Was the Christianity practiced here just a thin veneer over something older and more primal?

One journal entry caught his eye.

The archaeological team from the university arrived yesterday to examine the foundations. They claim they need to assess the structural integrity before the planned renovations, but I suspect they are looking for something. Dr Helgason mentioned pre-Christian artefacts, possible evidence of an ancient temple that once stood on this site and is now buried. I have tried to discourage their work, but they have official permission from Reykjavík.

The next entry was dated three weeks later:

The excavation has been halted. The workers reported hearing voices in the cave beneath the church, seeing lights where no lights should be. Dr Helgason packed up his equipment yesterday and left without explanation. The dig has been filled in, and the foundation stones replaced. Some buried things are better left undisturbed.

David flipped through the remaining pages, looking for more information about the excavation. He found only one additional reference, a brief note added in different handwriting:

The church was built here for a reason. The old religion runs deep. The silence is not empty.

The aurora returned that night, earlier and more intensely than before. David watched from the windows as green fire danced across the sky, but this time the light seemed to respond to something beneath the earth, pulsing in rhythm with vibrations he felt rather than heard.

There were geometric shapes in the aurora patterns that reminded him of what he had seen in the water earlier. The light moved with purpose, flowing along the walls and gathering near the altar.

David knelt in the front pew, trying to pray, but the words were hollow in his mouth. What if this place was not built to honour the divine, but to contain something that should remain buried? Something far older than his God.

And if the church was built to contain something, what would happen when that containment failed?

David shook his head suddenly, laughing at himself. The solitude was clearly getting to him, the lack of sleep over many weeks now, the tiny amounts of food he managed to stomach. Surely he was just on edge, his mind losing its tether to reality.

But even as the thought formed, David heard another sound.

Beneath the howl of the wind, a low scratching that came from below the altar.

And there, at the edges of his vision, shadows moved outside the windows. Not the chaotic dance of snow and wind, but deliberate shapes that seemed to flow like liquid darkness across the white landscape towards the church.

David paged back to the strange journal entry.

If the aurora comes on consecutive nights, and the earth trembles, and the sea shows patterns that mirror the sky, ring the bell to send what arrives back to the depths beneath.

As if summoned by the thought, a tremor ran through the ground beneath the church. The wooden pews creaked in protest, and David felt the vibration through his body where he sat. Of course, Iceland was a volcanic region, so earthquakes were common. Nothing to be alarmed by.

But combined with the strange aurora patterns and the shapes moving in the darkness outside, the tremor took on a more ominous significance.

The shapes beyond the windows were becoming more distinct now, and David pressed his face to the cold glass to get a better look.

Moving across the snow-covered lava field were figures that defied simple description. Not quite human in their proportions, not quite animal in their movement. They seemed to be composed of shadow and cold air, substantial enough to leave tracks in the snow but ephemeral enough that they shifted and flowed like smoke. Some looked like they had claws, and David thought of the gouges by the door.

The shapes moved with purpose towards the church.

David glanced back at the altar, which he now realised sat on top of a trapdoor. He could see the edges of it under the heavy table. What was down there? Did the shadows approach to release it from the depths?

More tremors shook the building, stronger now, from deep beneath the church foundations. The altar shifted a little.

David stumbled away from the window, his academic mind struggling to process what he was witnessing.

There had to be a rational explanation. Arctic storm mirages, perhaps, or his own hallucinations brought on by isolation and sleep deprivation.

But the journals. The warnings. The scratches on the door.

With hands that trembled from more than cold, David flipped through the pages of the journal with desperate urgency, looking for anything that might explain what he was experiencing.

Near the back, tucked between pages describing routine parish business, he found a folded letter.

To my successor in the sacred vigil—

If you are reading this, then you have begun to understand the true nature of our calling in this place. The church at Búðir was built by those who understood there are forces in this world older than Christ, older than the concept of faith as we understand it.

The missionaries who first came to this region studied the old records and spoke with the last practitioners of the ancient ways. They knew that beneath the Búðahraun lava field lay something that should not be awakened, entities that have slept since before the ice came, before humans walked this earth.

They could not destroy what lay beneath. Such beings are not subject to exorcism or holy water or the reading of scripture. But they could contain them, using the power of faith as a binding force. The church was built not to celebrate God's presence but to maintain His vigil against what sleeps beneath. The peal of the bell is not a call to prayer. It is a binding spell, maintaining the containment our predecessors established.

Each winter brings the test. The aurora calls to them, and they stir in their slumber. The bell must be rung, the vigil maintained. Not as an act of faith, but as an act of duty to all who would live in ignorance of what waits in the darkness, of what will roam the earth once more when we are gone.

Pray if you can. But ring the bell whether you believe or not.

—Pastor Bardur Einarsson, December 1834

David's hands shook as he scanned the letter. The temperature in the church had dropped even further now. Ice crystals formed on the windows, and his breath hung in the air like fog.

Another tremor shook the building, stronger than before, and David heard the sound of stone grinding against stone, as if massive blocks shifted beneath the church floor.

Cracks appeared on the stone floor, hairline fractures that spread outward from beneath the altar like a spider's web.

The shapes outside the windows multiplied now, flowing across the snow like an advancing tide of living shadow, moving with purpose toward the church. David could hear them calling with a sound like wind through hollow bones lying deep in ancient caverns.

Perhaps these creatures were here when the first humans crossed the land bridge into Iceland. When the Vikings arrived, and when Christianity stole the beliefs of the pagans. Perhaps they had endured the construction of the church above their land, but human civilisation, human existence itself, all of it was only a brief candle flickering against the vast darkness of deep time.

What was one man's grief over his wife's death compared to such immensity? What was one crisis of faith against the backdrop of geological epochs? Emma's cancer, his own spiritual struggles, the comfortable concerns of parish life, all of it shrank to insignificance in the face of beings that measured time in millennia.

The sound of stone cracking grew louder, and the altar began to tilt as the floor beneath it subsided. The ancient bindings were clearly failing, worn thin by time and starved of the faith needed to maintain them.

Ring the bell to send what arrives back to the depths beneath.

David stood frozen with doubt. How could one man, stripped of faith and certainty, stand against forces that had waited longer than human memory? How could the ringing of a simple bell banish entities that predated the very concept of worship?

He looked at the bell rope hanging near the altar, then at the cracks spreading across the floor, then at the shapes pressing against the windows with increasing urgency. The aurora blazed overhead in patterns that hurt to look at directly, and the temperature continued to drop toward levels that would soon make survival impossible.

David hesitated. What if he just let them come, let them reclaim what had always been theirs? They had waited beneath the ice and stone for eons before humans ever walked this frozen peninsula, and part of him yearned to surrender to that vast indifference, to let the darkness wash over him and end the grinding weight of grief that had followed him across continents.

It would provide the silence that had eluded him since his wife's death, and he could rest at last.

A sudden shaft of aurora light pierced the church windows, falling across Emma's gold cross where it lay beside his pillow.

She would not want him to yield. He knew it with every bone in his body. It would be a betrayal to give up the church while her spirit was still with him.

Perhaps faith didn't need to be about believing in God's love or providence or a divine plan. Perhaps it was about acting with purpose despite

God's silence, and maintaining the vigil even when meaning had been stripped away.

David reached for Emma's cross, his fingers closing around the familiar weight of gold against his palm. Her faith, if not his own, gave him strength.

He took hold of the bell rope.

He might no longer believe in God's love, and no longer find comfort in prayer or scripture, but he could still choose to act. He could ring the bell, not as an act of faith, but in the refusal to yield to ancient forces. Humanity still walked this earth and despite so much darkness in the world, it was worth saving for another dawn.

The rope was cold as iron in David's grip, and as he tugged it down, the bronze bell above pealed out across the ancient lava field, clear and defiant against the aurora-lit sky. The sound seemed impossibly loud in the frigid air, echoing off the glacier and rolling across the snow-covered stones like a challenge thrown at the feet of gods older than memory.

David clutched Emma's cross, holding onto what faith he had through her as he rang on.

The shadows drew back from the windows. Tentatively at first, but then faster, their forms dissipated into the snow, becoming one with the elements once more. The sound beneath the church quietened. The tremors stopped.

There was no logical reason the sound of the bell should drive these beings away, but perhaps it was just evidence that humanity still walked the earth, and that if a solitary human would still ring on the edge of the glacier, it meant the world was not yet ready for the end of time. And David rang on into the night.

* * *

The next day, when winter light finally dawned, David stood in the doorway of the Black Church of Búðir, one hand resting against the heavy frame. There were fresh claw marks next to the old, slashed deep into the wood, but whatever had made them was gone now, banished for who knows how long.

The ancient lava field stretched before him. Snow still covered the twisted basalt formations, but the shapes beneath appeared different now — not random geological accidents, but deliberate con-figurations. A story written in fire and pressure, in the slow dance of tectonic plates and the patient accumulation of geological time.

In the distance, Snæfellsjökull glacier loomed against the morning sky, its ice-crowned peak catching the pale sunlight and throwing it back in crystalline fragments.

David hefted the pickaxe he had found in a store cupboard and walked out behind the church. The small graveyard lay enclosed by a low stone wall that was barely visible beneath the snow. The head-stones were simple, made of weathered granite and basalt, carved with names and dates that marked the passage of human lives in this remote place. Names in Icelandic and Danish, dates spanning centuries, brief inscriptions in languages David couldn't read but whose meaning he could guess. *Beloved husband. Cherished daughter. Gone to God's rest.* Simple monuments to human love and loss, standing sentinel over graves dug into ground that was frozen solid for most of the year.

Near the centre of the graveyard, David found a space between older graves where the snow was shallow, where the ground might yield more easily to his efforts. He only needed a little patch.

He hacked at the ice-hardened soil.

As he dug, David felt something shift inside him. Not the return of faith as he had once understood it, but something deeper and more fundamental. The physical labour, the bite of cold air, the resistance of the ancient earth beneath his hands. It grounded him in a way that theological study never had. This was not about doctrine or scripture or the com-fortable certainties of seminary education. This was a connection to something vast and enduring, something that would continue long after his own fleeting existence had ended.

When the hole was perhaps eight inches deep — as far as the frozen ground would reasonably allow — David stopped digging and reached into his inner pocket. Emma's cross lay warm against his palm, the simple gold chain catching what little sunlight filtered through the overcast sky. She had worn it every day for thirty years, through their courtship and marriage, through illness and health, until the very end.

David held the cross for a long moment, sensing its weight. Not just the physical mass of metal and chain, but the accumulated weight of a lifetime of belief. Emma's faith had been simpler than his, certainly stronger.

He placed the cross gently in the shallow hole and covered it with the frozen earth he had excavated. At Emma's funeral, he had stood numb and hollow while others spoke of God's plan and eternal rest. Here, alone with the glacier and the sleeping things beneath, he felt something like peace settling into the spaces grief had carved out of him.

He was not burying Emma's faith. He was planting it here, adding her strength to the accumulated spiritual energy of generations who had worshipped in this place, who maintained the vigil, who held the line against forces that sought to reduce human existence to cosmic insignificance.

When he finished, David stood over the unmarked spot and looked out towards the vast glacier.

It watched from the distance, patient, eternal. The lava field stretched away in all directions, thousands of years of frozen fire bearing witness to one more day.

AUTHOR'S NOTE

The Black Church at Búðir is a real place on the Snæfellsnes Peninsula in Iceland, a few hours' drive northwest of Reykjavík. A church was established there in 1703 and the current church was built in 1848. There is a small graveyard next to it towards the sea, and it is still used for local worship and events. Any supernatural elements are, of course, fictionalised.

You cannot stay in the Black Church, but the wonderful Hotel Búðir is right next to it. We stayed there the night before my fiftieth birthday in March 2025 and visited the church on the day of my birthday. It is a truly special place in a starkly beautiful, remote area of Iceland, and as we drove away, the first inklings of this story came to me.

Snæfellsnes and the Snæfellsjökull volcano were the inspiration for Jules Verne's *Journey to the Centre of the Earth*, and also for Icelandic Nobel Laureate Halldór Laxness's novel *Under the Glacier*. Both wrote of the stark beauty and the sense of deep time you can feel on the peninsula. On this theme, I also recommend *Underland: A Deep Time Journey* by Robert Macfarlane, which provides a similar perspective on the insignificance of human life against the backdrop of geological time.

You can find Hotel Búðir at www.hotelbudir.is and more on the Black Church at www.budakirkja.is

You can read my trip notes and see my photos from five days in Iceland, including the Black Church and the aurora borealis at: www.booksandtravel. page/Reykjavík-northern-lights-iceland

BETWEEN TWO BREATHS

The sea, once it casts its spell, holds one
in its net of wonder forever.

—Jacques-Yves Cousteau,
Life and Death in a Coral Sea

London, England

RAIN HAMMERED THE GLASS walls of the Canary Wharf tower block, dissolving the city into a smear of grey and neon. Inside an office cubicle on the thirty-second floor, Naia Mitchells's monitor glowed aquarium-blue, leeching colour from her skin.

There were multiple tabs open on her dual screens: code bugs, angry emails, Slack messages from her manager. Another delayed launch, another promise that next week would bring some relief, if she and the team pushed just a little harder.

But it had already been eighteen unrelenting months, and Naia was drowning in work, gasping for air in the snatched hours away from her desk.

Tom from down the hall ducked into her cubicle. "Drink, Naia? You look like you could use one."

Naia looked up as rain lashed the glass with renewed energy. Thunder rolled somewhere beyond the limegreen safety lights. She imagined the Thames rising, swallowing each level one by one until there was nothing left but silence.

She nodded at her screen. "Deadline. Maybe tomorrow."

Tom walked away, and the voices of the team grew softer as the office quietened. Naia swallowed a couple of caffeine pills along with more painkillers. It would be enough to keep the headache and back pain at bay, at least for now. Her doctor had prescribed magnesium tablets, mindfulness apps, and a holiday she never managed to take. "You can't keep swimming forever," the doctor had said. "At some point, you need to take a breath, or your body will shut you down."

Another ping from Naia's email. Another error message in the code. An urgent buzz on her phone.

Panic swelled, pressing against her ribs. Her heart hammered — too fast, too loud. The office walls contracted, the ceiling pushed down. Her breath came in shallow gasps as her vision tunnelled. She gripped the edge of the desk, knuckles white, fighting the sensation that threatened to send her into oblivion.

Only one thing calmed her in this state.

She clicked open another tab, navigating to a travel site. A new article popped up: *Top Ten Dive Sites That Will Change Your Life.*

She zoomed into the photograph. Turquoise sky overhead, cobalt water below. Arches of volcanic rock framing shafts of sunlight that turned whirling schools of fish into stained glass. Naia's breathing slowed as she imagined floating alongside them, seeing only water and sky, leaving the stress of city life behind.

When the panic passed, she read the caption beneath the photo. The Poor Knights Islands, Aotearoa, New Zealand, named by the oceanographer Jacques Cousteau as 'one of the top ten dive sites in the world.' A place where she could breathe again. A place on the opposite side of the world, where she might escape the glass cage and digital chains that bound her to a life she could barely breathe through.

Naia pushed back her chair, shut down her laptop, and walked out into the rain. The water streamed down her face as she hurried home over the footbridge toward Poplar Dock. This river smelled of iron and industry, and the water was dark and forbidding. If there were any fish down there, she thought they must be mutated and eyeless, blind in the depths, unable to see the light.

She could join them.

A few stones in her pockets and all her stress would be submerged, forgotten.

She hesitated a minute on the edge of the bridge before walking on.

Back home, over a microwave meal, Naia clicked

back into the article, then researched how to get to Poor Knights Islands.

A flight from London to Auckland with just a short stopover.

A bus north to Tutukaka, a little port on the Northland coast.

A charter boat out to the islands.

She could swim in that blue sea by the weekend.

Lightning crashed outside as the storm hit in the darkness. Naia's hand hovered over the booking form. She took a slow, deep breath.

* * *

Tutukaka, Aotearoa, New Zealand — a week later

The marina smelled of diesel slick and sunwarmed kelp. The scent of yesterday's fish and chips still lingered in the air from the kitchens of the Deep Sea Angler's Club, further along the marina. Gannets wheeled overhead in lazy spirals, and on the weathered pylons, black shags spread their wings to dry. A pied oystercatcher stalked the shallows on bright orange legs, probing for shellfish with its blade-like bill, and below the surface, between the moored charter boats, a short-tailed stingray glided. Its spotted wings undulated through the clear water as it nosed along the sandy bottom, stirring up small clouds of sediment in search of buried crabs and worms.

Naia walked out of the dive shop, carrying a holdall bag containing a rental wetsuit, fins, and mask, with a weight belt over her shoulder. She followed the other tourists down towards the *Taniwha* waiting at berth twelve, as she tried to calm the nerves and anticipation in her fluttering stomach.

A young man stood at the bow, ushering the day's students aboard, ticking names on his clipboard. Under his fitted short-sleeved shirt, his arms were the colour of kauri bark, while the blond in his hair was salted almost white. Maori pattern tattoos spiralled from elbow to wrist, koru curls that evoked unfurling fern fronds and ocean eddies.

He waved Naia over. "Welcome aboard, I'm Matt."

"Hi, I'm Naia Mitchell."

He ticked her name off. "First time free-diving?"

She nodded. "I can hold my breath for maybe thirty seconds. On land."

"Don't worry," he said with a smile. "It's not about your lungs. It's about letting go."

As Naia joined the others on the boat, his words loosened the tightness in her chest. She was here to let go of late-night coding, fluorescent headaches, the constant stream of notifications and urgent messages.

Let go of her old life.

Let go of who she used to be.

Once everyone was onboard, the *Taniwha* chugged out of the harbour, beyond the lee of the headland out into the Pacific.

It was a calm day with gentle wind and waves, and in the distance, the silhouette of the islands drew closer with every minute. Two scalloped spines of volcanic rock rose from the water with a rugged tapestry of forest on top. Trees clung to every surface, their gnarled branches twisted by sea winds. Hardy shrubs and clumps of flax filled the spaces between, a testament to life's tenacity on these sheer cliffs, and as the boat drew nearer, Naia could make out dark mouths of sea-carved caves and arches, gateways to the world below.

The skipper moored the boat in a tranquil bay cradled by the island's steep cliffs. As he cut the engine, the sudden quiet was broken only by the gentle lap of water against the hull and the cry of a gull circling high above.

The water was a startling shade of turquoise, so clear Naia could see the kelp swaying over rocks fifteen metres below. The fronds swayed in the gentle current, catching shafts of sunlight as a school of blue maomao darted between the boulders.

"Everyone gather round," Matt called, his voice

carrying the calm authority of someone at home on and in the water. "This is Nursery Cove, perfect for beginners. Calm, shallow, protected from the swells. Today's about getting comfortable, learning to breathe properly, and seeing what's down there."

He demonstrated the most effective breathing technique for free-diving, his chest rising and falling in slow, deliberate waves. "Forget everything you think you know about holding your breath. This isn't about forcing air into your lungs. It's about relaxing into the water. Never push it. Never dive alone. Trust your body and have fun. Today is all about letting go."

Naia pulled the wetsuit up over her shoulders, the neoprene snug against her skin. The weight belt, necessary to get her past the initial few meters of buoyancy, settled around her hips with surprising heaviness.

As she adjusted her mask, she became aware of her breathing. It was no longer the shallow, panicked gasps of her London cubicle, but something deeper, slower. The salt air filled her lungs completely, each breath a conscious choice rather than a desperate necessity.

Matt came over and helped her adjust the weight belt. "Remember, the ocean wants to hold you. You just have to let it."

One by one, the group slipped over the side of the boat.

As Naia entered the water, the shock of the cold made her gasp, a jolt that cleared the last vestiges of jet-lag. It seeped through the neoprene, a creeping chill that was quickly replaced by a layer of warmth as her body heated the trapped water.

Following Matt's instructions, Naia rolled onto her front, face down in the water, and began her breathe-up, a specific way of relaxing the body and mind — deep, slow breaths in preparation for the dive.

The world above vanished, the sound muted to a distant hum. She focused only on the rhythms of her body.

With each long, controlled exhale, she felt the tightness in her shoulders dissolve. Her heart rate, which had been fluttering with nervous energy, slowed to a steady, deep beat.

She wasn't fighting for air. She was releasing it, letting it go, just as Matt said.

Just then, he sank past her, his lithe form perfectly streamlined, arms swept back against his sides, the koru spirals seeming to flow with the current. His long fins cut through the water with barely a whisper, propelling him down with an economy of movement. No struggle, no hurried descent, just a fluid, weightless fall toward the rocks below.

At the bottom, he glided between the kelp fronds with the grace of a seal, turning to wave up at the group with languid ease before beginning his ascent. No rush, no panic, just a gentle return to the surface world.

Naia floated, transfixed, as a deep longing unfurled in her chest — for Matt's skill, and also for the profound peace he clearly felt down there. She wanted to dive deeper into the water, deeper into herself, to find whatever it was Matt had discovered down in the blue depths.

There was only one way to get there.

Naia filled her lungs, folded at the waist, and tried to gracefully descend, but instead found herself flailing, her legs kicking frantically as she fought against her own buoyancy.

The weight belt wasn't enough to overcome her air-filled wetsuit and nervous energy, and she only managed a few meters before her body betrayed her, lungs burning with the desperate need for air.

She tried again and again, managing to get a little deeper, her ears popping as the pressure built. But her movements were heavy and clumsy, a world away from Matt's fluid grace.

Her heart hammered against her ribs, eating up precious oxygen. At maybe four meters down, panic crept in, a tightness in her chest, an urge to gasp.

But then, for just a moment, something shifted.

Her body stopped fighting.

The kelp swayed below her, and Naia experienced a fleeting sensation of perfect weightlessness, of belonging. For three heartbeats, maybe four, she glimpsed what Matt found down here.

Then her lungs screamed for air and she kicked hard for the surface, breaking through with a desperate gasp, treading water as she gulped down oxygen.

"Naia!" Matt swam over, concern creasing his features. "You okay?"

She turned to him, and despite the burning in her chest, despite her clumsy technique, she couldn't stop grinning. A wide smile that matched the one spreading across his own face.

"That was incredible," she panted, still catching her breath. "Can I go again?"

Matt chuckled. "We've got all day. Pace yourself."

As he swam over to help other students, Naia knew pacing herself would be impossible. The ocean had tilted her internal compass, and every arrow now pointed down.

As she repeated the breathing practice, ready to dive again, she gazed down into the blue. The shadows beckoned, and she tipped forward, chasing the call.

* * *

Four months later

Salt spray silvered the warped wooden boards beneath her bare feet as Naia unfurled her yoga mat on the hostel deck. Dawn light bleached the horizon pale gold, and the far off Poor Knights Islands rose from the Pacific, their volcanic silhouettes softened by morning mist.

Naia settled cross-legged, closing her eyes as she inhaled the cool morning air. Inhale for four… hold for seven… exhale for eight.

The breathing pattern flowed through her easily now, each cycle drawing her deeper into stillness. Her ribs expanded slowly, deliberately, no longer the shallow gasps that once kept her afloat in that glass tower back in Canary Wharf.

Here, breathing was meditation.

Breathing was ritual.

Breathing was preparation for the deep blue that called to her from beyond the reef.

Naia flowed through sun salutations as the light strengthened, her movements liquid and unhurried. The cramped hostel accommodation with its thin mattresses, shared bathroom, and walls that shook when the wind picked up would have horrified the woman she used to be. She had once measured worth in thread counts and postcode prestige, in the gleaming penthouse windows that reflected nothing but emptiness. Money for selling her soul, pixel by pixel. Luxury that was only ever a gilded cage.

And now this. A creaking deck, a second-hand yoga mat, a view of the islands that Cousteau himself had blessed. This was wealth beyond measure.

Here she traded her work in the dive shop for hours out on the boat, her physical labour for time beneath the surface. No shareholders, no deadlines, no fluorescent headaches.

Just the rhythm of tides and the promise of depth.

Naia slid into warrior one pose, feeling the strength of her muscles as she extended her arms out. Her hair had grown long and sun-bleached, no longer the sharp bob that framed her pinched, pale face back in London. Her skin, once translucent from office lighting, now held the gold of the Pacific sun and the kiss of salt spray. The old Naia existed only in photos on her abandoned social media accounts, a digital ghost trapped in a glass tower. This woman, stretching into the dawn with lungs that knew their true capacity, had shed that skin and emerged reborn from the depths.

By eight o'clock, Naia was crewing on the *Taniwha*,

helping Matt prep the gear while another batch of wide-eyed city workers clustered nervously on the deck. She recognised the pale skin, the expensive gear they'd use a couple of times, their phones clutched like lifelines back to the world they could only escape for a day. Their eyes held the same desperate hunger she'd once felt, that ache for something real beneath the artificial glow of urban existence.

"First time diving?" Naia asked a woman whose designer wetsuit in her gear bag still bore price tags.

The woman nodded, and Naia saw herself months ago, terrified, hopeful, drowning in her own life.

"It'll change everything," Naia said softly, stowing the woman's bag. "If you can just let go."

But she knew the woman would return to her cornered life, with only photos to show for her short-term escape. The ocean couldn't save every beaten-down office worker, but at least it had saved her.

Once anchored, Naia moved with practiced ease, checking equipment, explaining techniques. All the while, her eyes drifted to the water. This dive site was perfect for new divers, with a shallow protected area near the cliffs sloping out to deeper waters. Each clumsy dive reminded Naia of her own journey, but it was also a torment. She longed to slip beneath the surface, away from the noise of their nervous laughter, to find the perfect stillness that existed only in the depths.

During the surface interval lunch break, as the tourists clustered around a platter of sandwiches and fruit, Matt walked over with a smile. His fingertips brushed her wrist, a light touch, but electric in its familiarity. Their fingers intertwined briefly. A promise for later.

"You can go out for a bit now," he whispered. "I'll keep an eye on this lot. Just be careful. Don't go too deep."

"Thank you," she breathed, already reaching for her gear.

Naia tugged on the tight-fitting wetsuit and pulled out her long fins and mask, slipping into the water with barely a ripple.

She swam away from the boat, away from the shore, above the deeper water. She floated while her heart rate returned to normal and then began her breathe-up, preparing for descent.

The tourist chatter on the boat faded to whispers, then silence as she tuned out everything but the ocean beneath.

With each exhale, her heart rate dropped. The familiar calm spread through her limbs like honey from the wild bees on the cliffs above. The space between spaces, the threshold where surface thoughts dissolved and something older, deeper, took control. An ancient genetic memory resurfacing from when the water was home.

She filled her lungs, folded at the waist, and slipped under.

Her body streamed downward, arms swept back, legs together, the long fins propelling her with economical kicks that barely disturbed the water.

At five meters, the pressure began its gentle squeeze, compressing her wetsuit, making her heavier.

At ten meters, she stopped kicking entirely and surrendered to negative buoyancy.

This was the moment she lived for, this free fall through blue space, dropping through liquid light, weightless as a prayer.

The everyday world above dissolved.

Time dilated, stretched, became irrelevant.

Her lungs compressed to half their surface size, then less, but the mild hypoxia brought clarity rather than panic.

Colours shifted in the filtered light, the brilliant blues of the shallows deepening to midnight indigo.

A school of two-spot demoiselles parted around her like living water. She moved through them without urgency, each movement deliberate and fluid.

The urge to breathe remained distant, only a whisper.

At fifteen meters, Naia turned and began her ascent, following proper protocol even in the grip of blue euphoria. The return to light was a journey through shifting veils of colour — purple to blue to turquoise to the brilliant white-gold of surface sun.

Her heart rate picked up slightly as lighter pressure allowed blood to flow back into her limbs, but the profound calm remained.

Naia broke the surface in a controlled exhale, no desperate gasping, no panic. She turned towards the boat and made the okay signal, touching her fingertips to the top of her head. Matt waved back from the deck, grinning at her pleasure as she prepared to dive once more.

Later that evening, Naia nestled into the crook of Matt's arm, her damp hair still carrying the scent of open ocean, languid and content in the way that only hours in deep water could make her feel.

Around the table, the usual crew sprawled in mismatched plastic chairs — Jack, one of the skippers; Tui, a marine biologist who doubled as a dive guide; and Fred, a photographer whose underwater shots graced the walls of half the dive shops in Northland.

They sat on the deck of the Deep Sea Angler's Club wolfing down plates of battered green-lip mussels and steaming fish and chips, alongside cold bottles of Steinlager.

"Saw a pair of bronze whalers cruising the stern section of the Waikato today," Jack said in between bites. "Must've been four meters long, both of them. Gliding through those cargo holds like they owned the place. And the soft corals. Fred, the light was perfect. Pink and orange jewel anemones covering every surface."

Fred grinned. "I got some good shots at Blue MaoMao Arch today, swirling schools of koheru in shafts of light. I'll get them printed to sell in the dive shop."

"We mostly stayed shallow today," Matt said as he traced a lazy circle on Naia's shoulder with light fingertips. "Decent group of beginners. Naia's turning into quite the instructor."

She nudged him in the ribs. "Just following orders, boss."

He mock-groaned and the laughter of the group warmed Naia inside. Just a few months ago, she'd been a nervous tourist clutching rental gear. Now these locals accepted her as one of their own, and this place was beginning to feel like somewhere she could belong.

Tui took a long sip of her beer and then spoke, her tone serious. "I was down at Northern Arch, part of the biodiversity survey at depth, around thirty-five to forty metres. I was photographing these massive elephant ear sponges, absolute beauties, when I noticed something in the rock face. A gap, maybe three meters wide, cutting back into the cliff. It wasn't on any of our survey maps."

Naia felt Matt's arm tense around her shoulders.

"There was a current flowing out of it, and the water was colder, bluer…" Tui's voice grew soft and her eyes focused into the distance as if she could see back into that secret place.

"But it wasn't just cold. It was *alive*. The water moved like… like it breathed. And the light. It looked like the light was coming from *inside* the rock, not filtering down from above. Blue-white, like captured lightning, pulsing in rhythm with the current."

Tui shook her head, as if trying to dislodge the memory. "Maybe it was bioluminescence, but it wasn't plankton or jellyfish. It was the water itself, glowing from within."

"There's nothing down there," Matt said sharply. "You must have been narked at that depth."

"Or it was a way into the Cathedral." Fred's tone was quiet, almost reverent.

"What's the Cathedral?" Naia couldn't help herself, the question escaping her lips before she could stop it.

The others exchanged a look that carried years of shared knowledge and unspoken warnings.

"Legend," Jack said firmly, as he picked nervously at the label on his beer bottle. "Just a bloody legend."

"What kind of legend?" Naia pressed, curiosity overriding the growing tension at the table.

Matt pulled away from her, but he stayed silent as Tui explained.

"Some say there's a massive underwater cave system deep beneath the islands. Deeper than any diver has ever been, or could possibly go. There are local Maori stories about a sacred place where the spirits of the drowned gather, where the light coalesces into something rare and beautiful. Where the ocean keeps its secrets. To see it is to—"

"That's enough," Matt cut in. "It's a myth, and a deadly one, at that."

He pushed his chair back. "Naia, come with me. I want to show you something."

It wasn't a request.

Matt guided Naia away from the table, his hand warm in hers as he steered her out of the club toward the back of the marina complex.

Behind them, Jack launched into a raucous story

about last week's fishing tournament, clearly trying to change the subject.

"What was that about?" Naia said as Matt walked out toward a section of the waterfront she'd never explored. "What's the deal with this Cathedral?"

"This way." Matt led her around the back of the dive shop, where a narrow path wound between towering pohutukawa trees.

The lights and the laughter from the club faded behind them, replaced by the whisper of wind through native flax and the distant boom of waves against the headland.

Matt stopped in front of a maintenance shed tucked into a grove sheltered by overhanging cliffs. "We keep this hidden. Away from the tourists."

The obvious question — why? — died on Naia's lips as Matt unlocked the weathered door.

Inside, he fumbled for a moment before a soft light bloomed from within a carved pāua shell, its iridescent surface catching and amplifying the glow.

Naia's breath caught.

The shed wasn't for maintenance storage.

It was a shrine.

Photographs lined the walls, dozens of them, some recent, others faded with age and salt damage, some in colour and some black and white.

Faces smiled out from behind diving masks or raised beer glasses, eyes bright with the particular joy that came from spending days beneath the waves and on the ocean. But there was something final about the way they were arranged, something that spoke of memorial rather than celebration.

Against one wall, a carved piece of kauri wood held a collection of objects, like a rustic altar to an ancient sea god. A diving mask, its tempered glass spider-webbed with cracks and fused with barnacles. A speargun tip, its steel shaft corroded into something resembling delicate lace made of rust. A pair of lead weights melted and seared together by what could only have been incredible heat — or incredible pressure.

"As much as we love the deep water, Naia, it is not our domain." Matt reached out to touch each object, moving through them like rosary beads. "Depth is a debt. Oxygen is the currency. And those who forget pay the ultimate price."

The pāua-shell light cast shifting patterns across the weathered photographs, making the faces seem to move, to breathe. Men and women who'd shared her love of the deep blue, and lost their lives to it.

"Some were accidents — equipment failure, medical events, simple bad luck. But others..." He gently took her hand and placed it atop the fused lead weights.

The metal was impossibly cold, unnaturally heavy. Grief made solid. "Others went looking for something that shouldn't be found."

He turned to face her. "The Cathedral isn't a legend, Naia. It's real. It calls to those who love the depths, and its hunger knows no end."

The light in the pāua shell seemed to dim, or maybe it was just Naia's vision adjusting to the growing darkness outside. Through the small window, the marina lights twinkled like fallen stars, peaceful and safe and impossibly far away.

"Promise me," he whispered. "Promise me you won't go seeking the Cathedral. No matter what you hear, no matter how the deep water pulls you."

She stepped into his arms, pulled him close, put her head against his chest so she didn't have to meet his eyes. "I won't go looking." The lie tasted of salt and inevitability. "I promise."

In the early hours of the next morning, Naia walked outside to the deck and gazed out towards the islands. Somewhere beneath those dark waters, something vast and luminous waited — not just the Cathedral, but the truest version of herself, the one that could only exist in that impossible blue light. She practiced her breathing, slowing her heart rate, and felt the pull of the water, drawing her not down but home.

Behind her, through the thin hostel walls, she could hear Matt, restless in his sleep, his unconscious murmurs sounding almost like prayers.

* * *

Three weeks later

Naia slipped away from the dive boat while the tourists clustered around the crew for their lunch break. Matt was working in the dive shop on shore today, and as Jack was the skipper, he'd quickly nodded at Naia's request for some alone time. This was a more experienced group, and they were moored near Northern Arch, over the deeper waters.

As Naia finned towards the arch, she calmed her breathing. It was faster than usual from the anticipation that had been building since the night when she had first heard of the Cathedral.

Three weeks of careful diving, of staying within recreational limits, of pretending that Tui's words hadn't lodged themselves in her consciousness like a splinter of blue light.

Three weeks of lying beside Matt, listening to his peaceful breathing while her pulse raced with the thought of that impossible luminescence flowing from a crack in underwater stone.

Beyond Northern Arch, the sea floor dropped away in shades of blue. Even from the surface, Naia could see the rich ecosystem that thrived here in the temperate waters. Pink and orange jewel anemones clustered in every crevice, schools of blue maomao swirled through the arch like living ribbons of silver and indigo, and powerful kingfish hunted in the depths.

Naia adjusted her mask and relaxed, preparing to dive.

With each long, controlled exhale, her pulse dropped toward the meditative rhythm that marked the boundary between surface consciousness and the deeper state that free-diving demanded.

Her heart rate slowed, her peripheral vision sharpened. She was becoming something older, something at home in the blue depths.

She folded at the waist and slipped beneath the surface, her long fins propelling her with economical kicks, until she could surrender to the free fall through blue space.

The massive stone walls of the arch curved away on either side, carved smooth by millennia of current and wave action. The volcanic rock was alive with colour, jewel anemones swaying in the current like underwater flowers, purple and white sponges carpeting the walls, some of them massive barrel formations older than human settlement in these islands.

A school of trevally parted around her, their silver flanks catching filtered sunlight as they reformed in her wake. A massive snapper cruised past with lazy confidence, its scales catching the light like hammered bronze, before gliding away into the deeper blue.

Twenty-five meters.

Thirty.

The pressure squeezed her wetsuit tighter against her body, compressed her lungs, but Naia felt no urge to breathe. Her body found its rhythm in this liquid realm, her blood shunting from extremities to core, her heart rate dropping to something that barely qualified as life by surface standards.

Elephant ear sponges appeared on the deeper walls, their surfaces rippling in the current as they filtered microscopic life from the water, patient architects of calcium and living tissue that had been growing here for generations. Some were larger than dining room tables, their yellow and orange surfaces creating underwater gardens of impossible beauty.

Thirty-five meters.

Colours shifted in the filtered light, brilliant blues giving way to deeper indigo and purple. A stingray materialised from the blue distance, its wing-tips barely moving as it hung motionless, feeding in the current. Then more of them, stacked up in the arch, like a squadron in perfect formation, wings barely stirring.

Forty meters.

This was deeper than Naia had ever been alone, deeper than she should dive without supervision. But her body felt strong, her mind clear. The narcosis that should have clouded her judgment instead sharpened her focus to a laser point of awareness.

And there it was — just as Tui had described.

A crack in the rock face, perhaps three meters wide, cutting back into the cliff. A current flowed from the opening, carrying water that was colder and somehow more alive than the surrounding sea.

Blue-white radiance pulsed from within the crack, synchronised with the flow of the current. But it wasn't reflected sunlight or bioluminescent plankton. The light was generated from within the rock itself, as if the water glowed with its own inner fire. It pulsed in a rhythm that matched her slowing heartbeat, calling to something deep in her cellular memory.

Naia hung suspended in the water column, forty meters down and completely alone, watching light that couldn't exist paint the sea in colours that had no names. Mild hypoxia wrapped around her consciousness like silk — making every sensation more vivid, every moment stretch into crystalline clarity.

She should surface. Return to the boat. Pretend she'd never seen this impossible light flowing from the bones of the earth.

She finned gently toward the crack.

At the threshold, Naia paused and looked up. High above, sunlight danced on the surface, a world away from the deep.

She thought of Matt's fingertips tracing patterns on her skin, his voice whispering in the darkness of the shrine. 'Promise me.'

The light pulsed again, brighter now, and Naia slipped inside the crack.

It wasn't a choice anymore. It was inevitability, written into her DNA by millions of years of mammalian evolution, by the ancient part of her that remembered when the ocean was home and the air above was an alien place.

Naia finned on, propelling herself through the crack.

The rock walls enveloped her, worn smooth by eons of current flow, narrow enough that she could touch both sides with outstretched arms. As the current pulsed inward, it carried her deeper into the bones of the volcanic island.

The pressure should have been crushing, her wetsuit compressed paper thin, but Naia felt lighter than air. The light intensified as she was drawn deeper, no longer just emanating from the water but seeming to pulse from the rock walls themselves. The stone had taken on a translucent quality, as if lit from within by some impossible fire.

The passage opened out.

The Cathedral cavern stretched away into infinity, its walls curving upward and outward beyond the reach of her vision, disappearing into luminous darkness shot through with veins of living light.

Stalactites and flowstone formations hung like frozen waterfalls, their surfaces gleaming with the same inner radiance that suffused the water. The entire cavern glowed with bioluminescent fire — green and white and cobalt shifting and swirling in patterns that seemed almost like a forgotten language. The light moved in complex geometries of waves and spirals.

Schools of fish unlike anything she'd seen in the outer waters moved through the glowing medium, translucent creatures made of the same light that illuminated them. Some were familiar shapes rendered in luminescence: angelfish and wrasse and small sharks that glowed like living constellations. Others defied classification entirely, jellyfish-like beings that pulsed with their own inner rhythms, eel-like creatures that wrote sentences of light across the cavern walls with their movement.

Naia floated in the centre of the impossible space, her body weightless as her mind expanded beyond the boundaries of individual consciousness. Some part of her knew that narcosis had a deep hold now, but the euphoria was enlightenment rather than intoxication. She was seeing the world as it truly was, stripped of the illusions that made surface life bearable.

She understood now why others who sought this place had never returned.

They had evolved beyond the need for air, beyond the crude matter of terrestrial existence. They had become part of this flow, part of the living ocean that connected every drop of water on earth into a single vast organism.

A profound sense of coming home flooded her chest as Naia floated in the centre of liquid light. The last of her surface fears dissolved into the eternal blue.

This was where all the deep currents led, where every breath had always been meant to end. This was peace.

This was where she could let go.

AUTHOR'S NOTE

This story has a long personal history.

In March 2000, when I turned twenty-five, I was burned out and resigned my IT consulting job in London. I flew to Perth, Australia and spent months travelling, camping in the outback and exploring the country, as well as enjoying the Sydney Olympics.

I learned to scuba-dive in Fremantle, Western Australia, and my first PADI Open Water dives were on Ningaloo Reef further up the coast. I spent time on scuba-diving live-aboards on the Great Barrier Reef and dived at various places on the east coast of Australia.

By December 2000, I was ready to head back to the UK to start a new phase of my life, but I decided to travel around New Zealand first.

I flew into Auckland and immediately headed north, up to Tutukaka, to dive the Poor Knights Islands.

That first day on the boat, we saw whales lunge-feeding, pods of dolphins, and gannets dive-bombing into whirling balls of fish. Later that day, I saw blue maomao and schooling koheru in the arches of the Poor Knights. And I fell in love with the boat skipper, also one of the dive instructors!

In the months and years after, I dived the Poor Knights Islands many times, and became a PADI Dive Master. I even won an award for underwater photography, which you can see at www.jfpenn. com/koheru. That was back in the days of film cameras, even underwater!

I never free-dived, but I watched many of the free-divers with their long fins descending into the deep. I listened to them talk about how it felt to be so free. I longed for it and sought that euphoria myself.

While you're meant to always dive with a buddy, sometimes the experienced divers would head off alone. One day, I had the chance to do the same.

I was nervous and exhilarated as I descended alone to around forty meters, beyond where I should have gone.

I still remember the sheer joy of it. I felt the pull of the deep and considered staying down there, just breathing until there was no breath left.

That moment of consideration scared me deeply, and I realised I was suffering nitrogen narcosis, hypnotised by the beauty around me and forgetting how dangerous it was to be so deep, especially alone.

I checked my air and began my slow ascent.

I never dived alone again.

In 2023, I watched the documentary *The Deepest Breath*, which features the Blue Hole in Dahab, Egypt, where I also once dived. The idea for this story was born from that memory resurfacing, and written in honour of my many wonderful dives at the Poor Knights Islands.

I *absolutely* encourage safe scuba-diving and safe free-diving. Just make sure you follow all safety rules and precautions.

You can dive the Poor Knights Islands marine reserve with Dive! Tutukaka. Find out more at diving.co.nz.

If you'd like to *safely* free-dive, there are courses at freedive.co.nz.

I married the skipper, but (perhaps unsurprisingly) it didn't last, and we divorced a few years later. I wrote the poem on the next page, "Ocean Meditation," when I was ready to take my wedding ring off. It's a pantoum, a verse form in which certain lines repeat in a pattern, and it echoes elements of this story.

You can listen to a solo episode of my *Books and Travel Podcast* where I talked about scuba-diving and the wonder of traveling beneath the waves at: www.booksandtravel.page/scuba-diving/

I've written about other memorable dives in some of my other fiction. In *Stone of Fire*, Morgan Sierra recalls a dive at the Moeraki Boulders while inside St. Mark's Basilica. In *Deviance*, O's memory of an encounter with an octopus plays an important part in the story, and *The Dark Queen* features a dive to a submerged Egyptian city.

Books

Deep: Freediving, Renegade Science and What the Ocean Tells Us About Ourselves — James Nestor

One Breath: Freediving, Death, and the Quest to Shatter Human Limits — Adam Skolnick

The Deepest Breath, Netflix documentary — Laura McGann (2023)

OCEAN MEDITATION

Breathe out and you sink silently
Zen breathing, a calm mantra
In the clear blue, life is living
It matters not that you are watching
Zen breathing, a calm mantra
Slick silver scales scatter light
It matters not that you are watching
Down in the depths where vision fades
Sparkle silver scales scatter light
Drop your ring here, forget where it will lie
Down in the depths where vision fades
Some lonely monster will swallow your past
Drop your ring here, forget where it will lie
Colours cloak your present in glory
Some lonely monster will swallow your past
See how these tiny worlds survive
Colours cloak your present in glory
Look closer and see the universe in motion
See how these tiny worlds survive
You are more important than the least of these
Look closer and see the universe in motion
In the clear blue, life is living

You are more important than the least of these
Breathe out and you sink silently

Joanna Penn (2005)

BENEATH THE ZOO

Arania Webb stood alone before the padlocked gates of Bristol Zoo, her slender figure silhouetted against the wrought iron entrance of the Victorian ruin.

Early morning mist wrapped the derelict structure in gossamer, like an ethereal cocoon. The gates, carved with intricate vines and creatures of a forgotten era, creaked as a gentle breeze whispered secrets through the rusted bars.

Above her, the sky was a tapestry of grey, the early morning light catching the bare silver branches of the remaining trees that loomed over the zoo. Arania's gaze drifted upwards, following the twisted branches that stretched out like skeletal fingers, clawing at the heavens as if to escape their inevitable end.

She inhaled deeply, the scent of damp earth and decaying leaves mingling with a faint, almost forgotten musk of wild animals — or perhaps that was just the last vestiges of her memory. After all, this place was steeped in family history and a shadowed past that she only remembered in snatches.

Back when she was a child, Bristol Zoo had thrummed with life, the air filled with the calls of exotic animals, the delighted laughter of visitors, and the smell of spun sugar and cinnamon spice. Arania had walked these now-abandoned paths day after day with her father, the zoo's tracks like the strands of a DNA helix twisting and turning in patterns that bound them ever closer.

Dr Grafton Webb had worked as a conservation geneticist, responsible for the zoo's breeding program. When he wasn't traveling for research and speaking at conferences, he wove stories of distant lands and mysterious creatures into the specifics of scientific knowledge that he taught Arania as they walked the grounds.

"The zoo is not just a collection of individual enclosures and separate creatures. It is a living, breathing entity," her father would say. "Like a spider's web, it's intricate, strong, and resilient, but only if it is interconnected."

Even years later, Arania still pictured the zoo as a giant web, each path and enclosure a thread in a larger design. An ecosystem where every element, no matter how small or seemingly insignificant, played a vital role. The loss of one thread could unsettle the balance, yet the overall structure remained solid, adaptable in the face of challenge.

Those times together were more than just walks; they were precious lessons. Arania could see that now, although some would say Grafton's teaching bordered on obsession, even indoctrination. He constantly tested and extended her knowledge and innate spatial awareness, encouraging her to design and construct, to create structural order from chaos.

Perhaps he had been too harsh, and at times pushed her too hard, but that discipline had only benefitted Arania's career. Now she was the lead partner in a prestigious architectural firm, and the principal architect for the new build at the zoo site, one hundred homes in a residential quarter nestled in this historic area of Bristol. Once the old structures had been demolished, she would construct something truly beautiful here, a tribute to the old and a fresh start for a new generation.

Her architectural plans for the site blended organic, fluid curves with the geometric precision of spider webs, inspired by her frequent visits to the Insect House, where she would sit for hours watching orb weavers spin their intricate webs. Her father had carried a picture of her in his wallet, his little girl, cross-legged in front of the terrarium, the light from inside catching her unusual golden-ringed irises and her serious expression as she gazed intently at the creatures.

But it was not just the construction of their webs that held her attention; it was their predatory aspect that truly fascinated her. She observed how they would patiently wait, almost meditatively, for their prey to become ensnared in their silken traps. Once a victim was caught, the orb weaver's true nature would emerge.

Little Arania watched, unflinching, as they methodically encased their victims in silk, rendering them helpless. Beauty and horror intertwined, where one creature could live because another died. No moral judgment, just a natural cycle.

Her father's picture of her, gazing intently at the spiders, showed the inception of an architect who would build not just with physical materials, but with dark inspiration drawn from the natural world.

In the zoo construction, Arania would spin those ideas into reality, and her creative ambition would finally manifest in stone and glass. Her plans had already caught the attention of an esteemed architectural prize panel, and her career would accelerate once she shepherded the project into reality.

If only her father could see how far she'd come.

The sound of footsteps crunching on gravel came from the mist ahead and Ethan Vale walked out of the gloom, his lean, muscular frame clad in a bright yellow high visibility jacket, hard hat, and steel toe boots. He held a detonator in his hand, its red display clear in the morning's grey haze as it counted down to the final explosion that would level the site.

Ethan was the epitome of practicality and pragmatism, a seasoned site manager whose hands bore the callouses of hard labour, of his part in transforming abstract ideas into tangible reality.

Arania fleetingly thought of the nights they had spent together, when those same calloused hands traced the contours of her body with surprising gentleness. Their relationship was a tangle of mutual attraction and unspoken boundaries, where social class and Arania's unyielding ambition formed an invisible barrier. Their connection was strictly physical, devoid of deeper entanglements, which suited her, at least.

She smiled in welcome. "Morning. Is everything ready?"

Ethan's rugged features softened at the sight of her as he walked closer to the gate. "What are you doing here? The charges are set. The site's clear. We're on the final countdown to demolition."

He reached for her hand through the bars. "Are you sure you want to watch? I know how much this place means to you."

Arania took a deep breath, recalling the last day she had seen her father walking out of these very gates more than a decade ago. He had travelled to a remote region of the Congo Basin seeking some incredibly rare arachnid for his collection and never returned. Her mother had left while she was still a baby, but at least being without a family made it easier to concentrate on her career. Perhaps the destruction of the zoo would even close the chapter on her father's mysterious death.

She nodded. "I'm ready. I want to see the end of it all."

Ethan hesitated and then pulled out his phone. "Since you're here, there is one thing. I hesitate to bring it up, but we found something that wasn't on the plans — something underneath the Insect House."

He tapped through to a series of photos of a room Arania recognized right away — her father's lab.

His office had been in the Insect House, and he'd built a meticulously maintained lab on the basement level. Now, a wide crack zig-zagged down one wall. There should be nothing behind that wall but earth, but the photo clearly showed an open space beyond the crack. Within it, the light from the camera flash glinted on what looked like the bars of a cage.

Arania took his phone and zoomed into the picture. "What the hell?" It wasn't clear enough to see.

She frowned and bit her lip. They couldn't afford another day's delay, not after all the problems with environmental protestors at the site. They needed to detonate the main buildings today and begin clearing the blast site after it settled. She could not let this project get behind schedule.

But something about the hidden room gave her pause. She knew the building well, and this secret space was definitely not on the plans.

"We need to see what it is."

Ethan checked his watch and nodded. "We've got enough time. I can stop the detonation countdown if we need to. It won't take long and everyone else is off site, anyway."

He unlocked the padlock and pushed the gate open with a creak so Arania could slip inside.

They walked together through the shrouded ruins of the zoo, the absence of life a stark reminder of what had once been. The paths were overgrown, the enclosures empty. There was a haunting still-ness, as if everything that had ever lived here was dead and gone. It was reminiscent of an apocalyptic landscape, a place where the chaos of nature had retaken what humans had broken and remade in their own image.

They reached the Insect House, its once vibrant exterior now a faded echo of its former glory.

Ornate glass panels that had showcased a myriad of crawling and flying creatures were now cracked and covered with mould and moss, and inside, the once-vibrant terrariums lay barren. Gone were the tarantulas lurking in shadowed corners, and the iridescent beetles scuttling about with their glossy carapaces catching the light. There were no children with faces pressed against the glass, eyes wide with a blend of fear and fascination. Some of them no doubt grew into scientists, inspired by early curiosity about nature, while others shrunk back in terror, with decades of crawling nightmares ahead.

Ethan guided the way to the basement, his torchlight slicing through the oppressive darkness, illuminating the damp, mould-covered walls of what used to be her father's pristine lab. The musty scent of decay hung heavily in the air, so different from the sterile, orderly environment that Arania remembered.

This place, now shadowed and forgotten, had once been a sanctuary of wonder during her childhood. She had roamed its corridors with innocent delight, her father's hand in hers, his voice a comforting guide through the marvels of nature. Each day was a new adventure, each discovery a new treasure.

They reached the crack and Ethan pried away some of the loose bricks, widening it enough for

Arania to clamber through. He removed his hard hat and left it outside the wall in order to squeeze after her, and soon they were standing together in the hidden room. She had grown up here, yet she had never known of this place. What other secrets had her father kept?

The air was stale and smelled as if something had died here a long time ago. As the light from their torches flickered around the room, Arania took in the clutter of dusty equipment and scattered papers.

One wall of shelving was lined with jars filled with unidentifiable specimens floating in preserving fluid and covered with the grime of years. This place echoed the methodical layout of her father's official lab, but these jars gave her a dark sense of foreboding.

Arania reached up to one and wiped the dusty surface clear.

She jerked back in surprise and then leaned forward, tilting her head to one side as she examined the specimen more closely. A creature both beautiful and horrifying floated inside, a spider hybrid with what looked like human fingers in the place of its legs.

Each jar contained a different, twisted form. Some were small and malformed, their limbs at odd angles; others were larger, with almost human-like features distorted by arachnid traits. All were clearly failed experiments, aborted before they even drew breath.

There was a desk in one corner, next to a metal filing cabinet. An old backpack rested on the floor nearby, and above the desk was a pin-board covered with notes and charts, yellowed with age.

A photo pinned in one corner caught Arania's attention.

Her heart beat faster as she approached, recognising the child with the golden-ringed irises sitting cross-legged in front of a terrarium. This room was clearly her father's, but separate to his official lab, a place where he blurred the ethical lines of his official role.

Arania yanked open the desk drawer, sending up a cloud of dust as she rifled through the papers within. She pulled out a journal, opened it — and recognised her father's handwriting.

The notes were dated from years ago, just before the time of his last expedition. They detailed his research, not only into the conservation genetics he was known for, but into something far more unnatural.

There were more journals in the drawer, each marked with a year. She picked up another and rifled through.

Her father had chronicled his attempts to fuse arachnid with human DNA, creating chimeras that defied the laws of nature. There were diagrams of advanced genetic splicing, sketches of hybrid creatures, and notes scribbled in a frenzied hand. There was an edge of madness in her father's work, a glint of the passion that drove him to the chaotic edge of the Congo Basin, in search of a final key to what he sought to create.

But his experiments clearly transcended the boundaries of scientific ethics. As Arania read, she pieced together the narrative, her father's handwriting a map to the labyrinth of his mind. He had tried so many variations in his quest for perfection and, as she read, a dark suspicion grew in her mind.

Sketches and photographs accompanied the journal entries, visual records of her father's work. Images of creatures both beautiful and terrible, their forms a testament to her father's macabre genius. Among them, she found a series of drawings that detailed the conception and development of a unique specimen — a child with golden-ringed irises and the unique architectural abilities of an arachnid.

The sketches chronicled her growth from infancy, each stage of her development meticulously documented. Her father's notes were a mixture of scientific detachment and paternal affection, his pride in her abilities clear in his words. She was not just his daughter; she was the pinnacle of his dark creation.

Arania closed the journal, her hands shaking.

She could scarcely breathe.

The walls of the lab seemed to close in on her, the shadows lengthening into grasping fingers that clutched at her throat, choking her with the reality of what her father had done. His legacy was not one of scientific triumph but of ethical transgression, a dark web woven from the threads of ambition and hubris.

"Arania, you have to see this." Ethan's voice broke through her concentration.

She thrust the journal under some papers and spun around from the desk.

Ethan pointed to the far corner of the room, where a series of cages lay partially hidden under a tarpaulin. Next to the first cage, there was a surgical trolley laden with medical equipment — a bone saw, and scalpels of various sizes lying on a metal tray covered with dust. Standing next to it, a heavy cylinder of oxygen.

Arania walked over, her footsteps heavy across the dusty floor — and reached out with one shaking hand.

She pulled back the tarpaulin, stifling a gasp at what lay beneath.

Inside the cages were larger arachnid-humanoid hybrids, grotesque and yet somehow beautiful in their aberration. They were all long dead, husks of bone and fragments of chitin and dried flesh, yet Arania was seized by a sense of pity for the cursed creatures who had never had a chance at a real life.

In one cage, a skeletal figure sprawled awkwardly, its human-like skull attached to a spine that elongated into an arachnid exoskeletal thorax, the delicate structure of eight spindly legs radiating outward.

Another enclosure held a more distinctly human-shaped skeleton, with an abnormal number of jointed limbs, thin and fragile, scattered around the remains like brittle twigs.

In the final cage a small skeleton lay curled up, its form a blend of juvenile human and spider characteristics. The skull was mostly human, but with extra eye sockets, and the spine extended into a chitinous abdomen. The fingers of its skeletal hands were elongated, and the structure of the jawbone hinted at the adaptation of mandibles, a grotesque mimicry of a spider's mouthparts.

"What are these things?" Ethan's voice was a horrified whisper.

Arania crouched down and reached out to touch the bony fingers of the tiny skeleton. "An attempt to create life, to blur the line between species and take the best from both. They're my siblings in a way, born of the same ambition, the same twisted science."

Ethan stepped sharply away from her. "What do you mean?"

Arania looked up at him. "This was my father's lab. I think I was the only experiment that worked — and yet, he kept me a secret."

Ethan's expression changed to revulsion as he took another step back.

"It's okay, I'm still the same person." She reached out for Ethan's arm.

He flinched away, and she saw her future in his abhorrence.

If the truth were known, she would be considered an abomination, a creature less than human to be tested and experimented on. She would go from ascending the pinnacle of her architectural career to some black site for government experiments. She could see the future spin out into a web of her father's origin, weaving into the tapestry of fate.

There was only one solution.

"We need to get out of here. Now." Ethan turned to leave, his movements stiff, his expression a stony mask.

Arania's heart raced. She couldn't let him go. The truth could not escape these walls. Her career — her very life — everything she had worked for would crumble if he revealed what he had learned. She couldn't take the risk.

As Ethan took another stride towards the exit, Arania reached for the heavy cylinder of oxygen next to the surgical trolley.

Driven by instinct, she wrapped her hands around the cold metal.

In one swift, desperate movement, she swung the oxygen tank with all her might.

It connected with the back of Ethan's head with a sickening thud. His body crumpled to the ground, motionless.

Arania stood frozen, the oxygen tank still in her grip, her breath coming in ragged gasps.

She dropped the tank, the clang of metal against concrete echoing in the room. Her breath hitched, her hands trembled, tears sprang to her eyes. What had she done?

She knelt beside Ethan, her hands hovering over him, afraid to touch his wound, afraid to confirm what she feared. There was blood, a dark pool spreading across the dusty floor — but his chest still rose and fell with shallow breaths.

He was alive. She could still save him.

She could run outside, call for help, stop the demolition… But what then?

She would be an attempted murderer as well as a genetic aberration. Her promising future would be ruined.

Arania played out the alternate scenario.

The detonation countdown would continue. No one even knew she was here. If Ethan was lost in a terrible accident on the site he managed, she would cry in front of the police, mourn his loss, and then — after a suitable period — she could resume the project.

She stood up and looked around the lab, at her father's sanctuary of dark secrets, at everything he worked so hard for. She was his most successful creation. He could have cemented his own shining future in genetics by revealing her presence, but he had given everything to protect her. She would not wreck it all.

Her hands were steady now. She wiped her eyes and took a deep breath.

One creature could live because another died. No moral judgment, just a natural cycle. Perhaps that which was arachnid inside her had reared up to defend its territory? Perhaps there might be other gifts she could realise given time — and experimentation.

But for that future to play out, she had to make sure Ethan never returned to the surface.

The detonator lay on the floor where it had fallen from his hand, the red numbers still counting down. There were only ten minutes before the whole place exploded and collapsed around them.

Ethan moaned and stirred a little, reaching out his fingers towards her.

Arania picked up the oxygen cylinder and — without a second's hesitation this time — slammed it down on his head.

The pool of blood grew.

He stopped moving.

The blunt force trauma reflected exactly what happened here. Ethan had been caught in the explosion and lumps of masonry crushed the life from him. After the demolition, when the site team realised he was missing and came looking for his body, they would find him broken and shattered down here.

There would be nothing to implicate her — as long as she cleared any evidence of her family connection.

Arania grabbed the old backpack and stuffed her father's journals inside, along with the photo from the pin board.

As she counted down in her mind, she hurried

to the crack in the wall through which they had entered and clambered out. Every second was precious.

Her sprint back through the zoo was a blur. The mist seemed to swallow her as she dashed for the last time along the overgrown paths, past the empty enclosures that once teemed with life.

Arania reached the gates and slipped back through to the other side, padlocking the gate once more.

She stood there at the threshold of freedom and captivity, her breath coming in short gasps. For a moment, she wished she could wind the clock back and see Ethan walking out of the mist once more.

But it was too late. There was only one choice now.

Her father's failed experiments would be destroyed along with the derelict buildings. The corpses of those he created would be buried beneath the zoo, reducing his twisted legacy to dust and memory, and no one would ever know.

Arania hurried to her car and drove away from the zoo, counting down the seconds to detonation in her mind.

The road wound up to a hilltop on the Downs behind the zoo, the opposite direction from the site office and a safe distance away with a clear view of the impending destruction.

The morning air was cool and crisp as Arania stepped out of her car and walked to the edge, looking down at the zoo below, its structures eerily quiet in the moments before their end.

As the final seconds ticked away, a profound silence enveloped the area.

The charges detonated.

The ground trembled. A deep rumble resonated through the air.

A billowing cloud of smoke and dust rose as the old buildings succumbed to the chain reaction of the explosion.

Arania watched, her eyes wide, as the structures collapsed in on themselves, one after the other.

As the last of the structures fell, a massive plume of smoke rose into the air, dark and foreboding, and Arania thought she saw the lines of a web form, before the smoke dissipated in the morning breeze.

AUTHOR'S NOTE

My parents divorced when I was young, and when my dad came to visit me and my little brother in Bristol, England, he would take us to the zoo. It had enough going on to keep two kids occupied as well as treats to bribe us, and botanical gardens to run off the sugar high before he dropped us home.

Because of these memories, Bristol Zoo is a nostalgic place for me. I associate it with a difficult time when I didn't know how to relate to my dad, but at least we could walk around and look at the animals. Those were precious hours together.

In November 2020, the BBC reported that Bristol Zoo would relocate to a new site, and it closed down in September 2022. In April 2023, the BBC reported that the old zoo would be demolished and 196 new homes built on the site, with the botanical gardens remaining open to the public once completed.

When I heard the news, I couldn't help wondering what might be discovered underneath the foundations of the old Victorian zoo, and what if the architect in charge of the project had conflicting emotions about the place? Something about her father, perhaps…

During the summer of 2023, I finished a long-term non-fiction project, *Writing the Shadow: Turn Your Inner Darkness Into Words*, and in it, I reflected on the shadow of divorce and family relationships.

I wrote this story to integrate the past and close the emotional loop on Bristol Zoo as it begins its reinvention.

The name Arania is Persian and means 'spider,' but it's also associated with ambition and professional success.

If you enjoyed this short story, you might also like my crime thriller *Desecration*, as British detective Jamie Brooke investigates a murder that resonates with the dark history of anatomy and the genetic engineering of monsters.

Related links

"Bristol Zoo to leave Clifton site after 185 years," BBC News, 27 November 2020 — www.bbc.co.uk/news/uk-england-bristol-55103745

"Bristol Zoo: 196 homes to be built on former site in Clifton," BBC News, 26 April 2023 — www.bbc.co.uk/news/uk-england-bristol-65388960

SOLDIERS
OF GOD

THERE WAS A CHILL IN the winter air, but fires still burned south of the city and smoke drifted over the spires of the Vatican as Martin Klein walked by the River Tiber in the dawn. Italian public services were so under-funded that municipalities allowed the burning of rubbish, perhaps hoping that the noxious fumes drifting over government buildings in Rome would spur action. But all it did was cast the city in an eerie haze.

Crimson and burnt orange from the fires bled into the clouds, so the holy city seemed aflame. Some read it as an omen heralding divine judgment, others a reflection of the pyres of hell. All Martin saw was the sublime accomplishment of man's architectural genius, threatened by humanity's equally accomplished methods of destruction.

He was alert to the sound of the city waking as he headed west along a street of graded cobblestones. The *putt-putt* of scooters, the blaring horn of a taxi as it navigated the claustrophobic streets, the barking of local dogs protecting their territory.

Most of the shops were still shuttered with shaded windows overlooking the street, but as Martin passed a *panetteria*, the sound of clanging echoed from inside. As the baker pulled out the loaves for the day, the scent of fresh bread and the sweet notes of vanilla cannoli wafted out into the street. Martin couldn't resist. He slowed and searched his pockets for spare euros. Finding a note, he ducked into the bakery and bought a warm cornetto, fresh from the oven. He munched the flaky pastry as he walked on toward the Vatican, enjoying the sweetness in his mouth. It would be ample fuel for his morning's search.

Martin was on loan to the Vatican from ARKANE, the Arcane Religious Knowledge And Numinous Experience Institute, which specialised in solving religious and supernatural mysteries around the world. He was the Head Librarian and Archivist, but this impressive title did not encompass his ability to find patterns in digital chaos or help ARKANE agents find clues during their global missions.

A senior cardinal had requested Martin's help to create an AI-enhanced search engine that would use natural language processing to automatically tag and catalogue the ever-growing Vatican archive. It had been scanned over the last decade — millions of crumbling pages turned into bits and bytes to make it easier to find hidden scraps of knowledge lost for centuries.

But it turned out that scanning made it even harder to find anything.

While the aged librarians had known where to physically locate long-forgotten tomes, and obscure academics had deciphered faded labels in the miles of stacks, now a rule-based search algorithm directed the curious to their answer — but only those skilled enough at asking the right questions could find what they were looking for. Martin's job was to figure out a way to make it easier for human minds to work with the computers, to turn the priests of Vatican City into AI-assisted researchers, to bridge the gap between machine and man. He would create threads of crimson light through a labyrinth of words and enable new understanding from old knowledge.

Martin reached the entrance and passed through the extensive security at the door of the Vatican Apostolic Archive, formerly known as the Secret Archive. The previous title proved to be catnip for conspiracy theorists and the new, more mundane epithet kept them at bay — although its secrets remained just as potent.

Martin wound his way through the twisting corridors lined with stacks of shelving, piled high with books and manuscripts and rolls of vellum. Others might have stopped to examine some obscure text to see where serendipity might lead in this storehouse of buried wisdom, but Martin was blessed with extreme focus. It went along with his brilliance at mathematics and coding, his difficulty in fathoming people's behaviour, and his dislike of being touched. Some labelled and medicalized such personality traits, but Martin chose to believe that everyone was on some spectrum or another. As long as he proved useful to ARKANE, he was happy.

His temporary desk was at the back of a tiny storeroom where he could work uninterrupted, his fingers flashing over the keyboard as he roamed the vast digital landscape. The Vatican scanning project had initially set him up in their open plan area, but Martin couldn't work with all those people, all that noise, all those interruptions. It was better here in the quiet, with only his three enormous screens to focus on.

He sat down, flexed his fingers, rolled his shoulders, and dived back into the emerging algorithm.

There was an alchemy in the dance between human and machine. Martin thought of it as a dance because it was ever-moving, ever-changing, ever-responsive to the new stimuli he provided. The powerful artificial intelligence engine would be nothing without Martin directing it. It had no purpose of its own, no will to discover, no need to work. But once he instigated the dance, it would follow, then leap ahead into something unexpected, before Martin took it in another direction. Working together, they would discover something new. The process was addictive in its creativity.

A half smile flashed across his face as the machine found a commonality between a medieval treatise and a postmodernist essay on liberation theology, a link no human mind would have discovered since the documents originated half a world apart and in two different languages. Martin was training the algorithm to find such relationships across time and space, language and format, and even encouraged the machine to examine heresies long repressed.

He had started with a copy of the code he created at ARKANE to synthesise their vast knowledge base, a system he had worked on for years since being recruited from the University of Cambridge with a Doctorate in Computer Science and Archaeology. He had been at the job for years now and while delight was almost a daily occurrence as he drove the AI to new heights, it took a lot to surprise him.

But even Martin was surprised by what he found later that day in the Vatican online archive.

It was a scanned copy of a papal bull, *Militia Dei*, Soldiers of God, issued in 1145 by Pope Eugene III, allowing the Knights Templar to take tithes and burial fees. It also decreed that the Templars should bury their dead in their own cemeteries. The paper was crumbling, the handwriting faded, the Latin barely readable in spindly letters, although the pope's signature and seal were clear enough.

This bull, along with certain others, had been the basis of Templar wealth in medieval times — and the bull in itself was not unusual. Popes had issued such edicts since at least the eleventh century. But whoever processed this document had scanned another alongside it in the same batch, and it was the second document that made Martin's eyes widen as the AI engine translated it from Latin.

This kind of mistake was not unusual in archival projects. Scanning could only be done by hand and much of it was completed by enthusiastic students, lay brothers and sisters, and other temporary staff. Although most began their task with a keen attitude, determined to abide by the correct procedures for handling such documents, the work quickly became repetitive and tedious. It was no intellectually romantic job where the curious could stop and revel in their proximity to history, and there was no time to read every document.

Each page had to be placed carefully on a glass screen and scanned or photographed.

Hour after hour.

Day after day.

While millions more pages lay waiting to be processed in boxes and files and books and stacks and corridors and buildings across the world of the Catholic Church. It was enough to make any archivist lose focus and accidentally scan two pages together. This extra document must have lain near the papal bull in the day's papers and should have been scanned separately. And yet it was here, and it hinted at something quite unusual.

Martin leaned closer to the screen and read every word of the document, then reread it while checking the Latin against a separate translation engine open on another screen.

It was correct. There was no doubt of its meaning and yet, he could scarce believe what it suggested.

Martin might once have merely reported this anomaly to the Vatican Head Archivist and left it at that, proceeding with his job with no further thought of the mystery.

But in the last few years, he had joined agents Jake Timber and Morgan Sierra on several missions, and Martin found himself tapping into a vein of curiosity that ran deep within those who found their home at ARKANE. There were mysteries in the world buried under lies obscured by history, all designed to hide from humanity the truth that there was more to the world than could be seen on the surface.

Martin frowned and tilted his head to one side as he considered his options. It seemed sensible to confirm the truth before taking any further action. He needed to see the original document.

He pushed back his chair, its legs scraping on the stone floor, and as he mentally re-entered the physical world, Martin realised the day had passed in a blur. The sounds of the main archive room were quieter now, as the team had mostly left already.

Martin walked through and approached Bishop Giovanni Sandri, who headed up the archiving project and often sat at his mahogany desk until late into the night. He was thickset, with a bulbous red nose and broken veins around his cheeks, a priest who looked his age indeed, perhaps sent down here to serve out his final years. His blue eyes brightened as Martin approached.

"Have you found something of interest, my son? You so rarely join us. It must be fascinating indeed."

Martin bobbed up and down on the balls of his feet, running his fingers through his shock of blonde hair, spikier than usual since he hadn't cut it in a while. "I need to see the original papal bull, *Militia Dei*. Where is it?"

Bishop Sandri chuckled, and Martin presumed it was something to do with his abrupt manner, but he had given up trying to understand the niceties of polite human interaction. Better to do his job so well that people forgot anything but his excellence.

The bishop opened a large ring binder on his desk and sifted through the pages, peering down at the handwritten scrawl through reading glasses as he ran a finger down the side of the page.

Martin tapped his foot on the floor as he tried to control his impatience. It was hard to believe that this digital project was still managed on paper.

After a minute, the bishop looked up. "It was scanned two weeks ago. The original will be back in the temperature-controlled vault. Section 27C in the sub-basement under the sculpture gallery."

Martin tilted his head to one side as he accessed the location in his mental model of the labyrinthine Vatican corridors. "What about anything scanned at the same time? Would that be archived in the same place?"

The bishop nodded. "Yes, I should think so. At this point, we're racing against time to scan the older material before it crumbles to dust. The impact of climate change on the original archives was never considered." He shook his head and sighed. "We're all running out of time, Martin."

But Martin was already half out the door and down the corridor, the bishop's words muted by the stone that had witnessed time passing with each generation.

Martin left the archive workrooms and headed up and out across a stone plaza, surrounded by cloisters. Low hedges bordered gardens of herbs and aromatics, used by the Vatican chefs and those who might once have been called apothecaries. It was dusk and the scent of rosemary and sage filled the air. Swifts darted high above, spiralling in the gathering dark as they devoured insects on the wing.

Martin entered another corridor and strode along to the sculpture gallery with its strange combination of classical poses and ecclesiastical art. The Vatican walked a tightrope between venerating the beauty of the human physical form and hiding it away for fear of what dangerous emotions it might arouse. This gallery was one of many places where statues were placed when they fell on the wrong side of the line.

He hurried down the spiral staircase into the vaults beneath, some of which were supposedly temperature controlled. But this warren of rooms was part of an ancient electrical system that took more than its fair share of power, and often the lights flickered on and off. Martin suspected that the temperature was merely controlled by nature of it being underground.

He found his way to Section 27C, pulled on a pair

of white cotton gloves, and searched the stacks for the papal bull and its unusual literary companion.

Eventually he found a drawer with the papal bull pressed between glass to keep it flat. It was written on papyrus, the material yellowed with age. Despite its unprepossessing appearance, Martin found it a pleasing piece of history — but not what he was looking for.

He searched in the drawers on either side, carefully lifting out old pages and sifting through manuscript fragments. It was a glimpse of how useless this knowledge had become hundreds of years after monks copied these pages. Only someone physically in the room could learn from them, and only then if they could find specifically what they wanted in the first place. If the digital transformation of the Vatican Archives was successful, its real power would be unlocked by scanning, and its ancient knowledge surfaced by his AI engine. Time was indeed running out, and Martin wondered how much more knowledge was kept impenetrable across the world by the physical prison of books.

He turned to an oversized leather folio and, as he lifted it, dust rose around him with the musty smell of mould. There was a document in the front on the cotton rag paper used by the archive team as it was acid free. It noted the retrieval and scanning date — two weeks ago.

Martin's heart raced a little faster. The extra document had to be here. He turned the pages carefully — and there it was.

He reached out and gently placed his finger on the page. Even through the glove, Martin could sense the brittle texture underneath. He spent so long viewing the world through a screen, it was a singular experience to be physically engaged with words inscribed on parchment so long ago. Despite the clear advantage of the digital format, even he had to acknowledge that nothing beat seeing these archaic documents in their original form.

He read the ancient words, translating the Latin written by the hand of a long-dead cardinal who served a long-dead pope back when it was much easier to keep a secret, even a significant one such as this.

The letter explained why the Knights Templar needed separate graveyards and contained detailed instructions on how particular knights from a particular area of France must be buried.

They should be laid within heavy metal coffins that could withstand pressure from outside — and from within.

The corpses must be bound with strong leather straps, as those used to drive oxen on the plough, and secured by powerful hooks to the coffin sides.

Then the final line, the one that gave Martin pause.

Metal spikes must be driven through the hearts of the *militia dei*, the soldiers of God.

He blinked and let out a slow breath.

The papal bull had clearly disguised these specific requirements by giving the Templars private burial grounds. They could do what they needed to in secret without others in the church and the wider community knowing. But the instructions led to only one conclusion about the nature of these soldiers, and it seemed impossible to consider what that might mean.

Martin read the rest of the document. The group of Templars referred to had lived in a particular area of Paris. He pulled out his phone and checked the online historical maps. It looked like the graves were buried deep under the cobblestones of what was now the Marais district.

With proof that the document was indeed real, Martin considered reporting it to ARKANE Director Marietti so field agents could investigate further.

But this was a footnote in history, not some emergent risk.

ARKANE agents usually had to race against time to stop some terrible threat of destruction, but there was nothing here except intellectual curiosity. His report would get nothing more than a note in yet another archive — unless he went to check it out himself and determined whether it was worth investigating further.

It was only a short flight to Paris, and Martin had a good excuse at the ready. He could use the trip to clarify some questions about the materials used for the older Vatican documents, the weave of papyrus and whether it could be aged or even traced to a specific geographic area. There just happened to be a biblical scholar in Paris with a specialism in paleo-botany, the evolutionary history of plants and the biological reconstruction of past environments.

Professor Camara Mbaye worked at the Bibliothèque Nationale, when she wasn't visiting Sir Sebastian Northbrook in London. The two had met in Senegal many years ago and rekindled their old friendship during the mission to find the Tree of Life. Since Sebastian was one of Martin's closest friends, he had recently spent time with Camara. He respected her deep knowledge — and her patience with his endless questions.

Martin would once have said he was a happy loner, preferring to lose himself in code rather than conversation. But over his years at ARKANE he had found true friendship, forged in the fire and blood of active missions. Jake Timber, Morgan Sierra, and Sir Sebastian Northbrook — all had come to his aid in the past, and all would help him now. But Sebastian was busy curating an exhibition at the John Soane Museum, Jake was occupied on a mission in Vienna, and Morgan was researching something about blood curses in the ARKANE library back in Oxford. She had been in a dark mood since returning from Northumberland, and she was meant to be in Vienna with Jake, anyway. He didn't want to disturb her.

Camara was no field agent, but she was a scholar with deep intellectual curiosity — and she knew Paris. The Marais district wasn't far from the Bibliothèque Nationale, so perhaps she would at least join him for a coffee.

As Martin walked back out of the Vatican, he texted Camara and asked her to meet him tomorrow morning in the Marais to discuss the history of the Templars in Paris. He hinted at a mystery but didn't give any details.

Within minutes, Camara replied in the affirmative, and as the rubbish fires lit the Roman night sky with crimson flame, Martin wondered what he might find in Paris tomorrow.

* * *

It was a civilised ten a.m. by the time Martin walked along Rue de Bretagne toward the café where he would meet Camara. There was a touch of drizzle in the air and the pale winter sun hid behind dark clouds. Despite the cold, Parisians sat sipping coffee under café awnings, coats pulled tight around them, some swaddled in blankets left by café owners to encourage custom. One elderly man read the morning paper, his head almost buried in the over-sized pages. At a table nearby, a young woman with old eyes smoked a cigarette as she stared out at those hurrying past, her coffee steaming in front of her.

The city of Paris had seen so much and the river of history was ever moving, but even in these modern streets, Martin found evidence of the Templars. He walked past the Hôtel Jacques de Molay, named after the final Grand Master of the Order, burned alive in front of Notre-Dame Cathedral in 1314. He turned around one side of the Square du Temple, a garden built over the ruins of a huge medieval Templar fortress. It had been used in the French Revolution to imprison the royal family before their bloody execution on the guillotine, then destroyed by Napoleon after it became a place of pilgrimage for Royalists. Now it was known for its Metro station near a covered market and courthouse in the third arrondissement, although there were traces of modern tragedy, too.

Martin walked past a memorial to the Jewish children aged between two months and six years who had lived in the area before being deported to Auschwitz and murdered in the gas chambers in the early 1940s. He considered how much blood had soaked into the soil of this garden. The trees were bare now, their limbs reaching in supplication toward heaven, but in the summer they would be lush and green, providing shade for children once more with no thought of past atrocities. History turned another page, and the next generation would no doubt find different ways to torture one another.

It was ever thus.

As Martin turned the corner around the edge of the square, he spotted Camara sitting at a table in front of the Tour du Temple café. She was reading something on her phone, her frown deepening as she concentrated on some vexing problem. She wore a tailored trouser suit in pale forget-me-not blue, which offset her dark skin perfectly, and a neck scarf with a touch of crimson in the weave. Camara was slender in the way that French women seemed to master, and her profile was regal. While she had become Parisienne in the decades since leaving Senegal, Camara would always be a proud African.

She turned and smiled at Martin's approach, rising

to kiss him on both cheeks in the French way of *la bise*. Despite his usual aversion to touch, Martin had grown used to Camara's natural greeting, and he didn't shy away, although he had never learned to return the kiss. Perhaps one day he would master the art, but for now, it was enough to tolerate it.

"*Bienvenue à Paris*, Martin. It was so lovely to hear from you."

Camara waved at the waiter to bring them both coffee and they sat facing the street as Martin explained what he had found in the document.

He showed her an image on his phone of the Latin text. Camara leaned closer to examine it, zooming in on the screen as she read, her academic Latin no doubt better than Martin's own. He took the chance to drink his coffee, served in the French style in a tiny cup. It was only a few mouthfuls, but every sip was perfection.

Camara put the phone down, her eyes bright with interest. "So you think the tomb might still be buried under this area?"

Martin nodded. "The document indicates that the burial place of these particular knights was *below* the crypt. It might have been concealed by the destruction of the fortress, so perhaps it is still down there."

Camara shook her head and smiled. "We have

both seen strange things indeed, *non*, so why should this be any different? In fact, when your text mentioned the Templars, I did some digging and chose this café because of its location."

She pointed at the church across the road. "That is the Église Sainte-Élisabeth de Hongrie, Saint Elizabeth of Hungary. Its crypt has the deepest foundations of any building in the area of the original Templar fortress."

Martin looked beyond the parked cars and scooters at the church. In a city dense with imposing architecture and famous landmarks, it was nothing much. Perhaps it might have been notable in a smaller city, but here, pedestrians walked past without a second glance.

The classical facade was of Jesuit design with Doric columns flanking the entranceway. A pietà sculpture of Christ in the arms of his mother was positioned above the door, and statues stood in niches on either side. It was unremarkable — and yet, secrets were best kept in places where curiosity was not easily aroused. The boring and mundane sometimes hid the most extraordinary.

Camara opened her phone and tapped at the screen, turning it so Martin could see a picture of a fossilised leaf. Not really his expertise, but squarely within Camara's paleo-botanical domain.

She grinned. "Isn't it beautiful? It's a *Ginkgoites huttonii*, Middle Jurassic. I helped identify it for a friend at the Société Botanique de France who is also a bell ringer here at the church. They have a lot of concerts because of the incredible acoustics. I messaged him after you contacted me, and he's cleared us with the organ master who is in there practicing right now, so we can go have a look around."

They finished their coffee and crossed the road to the church. Camara led the way inside, and as they walked through the nave, the peal of the organ rang out in the exquisite strains of the Magnificat canticle.

Although Martin did not adhere to any particular religious faith, he found a satisfaction in sacred music. It resonated with his mathematical sense of the world and he appreciated the beauty in its order. As Camara navigated her way up to the organ loft, Martin stopped near the choir stalls to listen and examine the church.

Elaborate frescoes of recognisable biblical scenes including the Beatitudes and the Last Judgement decorated the nave. As the clouds parted outside, weak rays of sun shone through stained glass windows portraying John the Baptist and John the Evangelist, their expressions forever caught between suffering and glory. There were Stations of the Cross around the church for the faithful to worship at on holy days and a chapel on one side dedicated to the Virgin Mary. It smelled of candle wax, incense, and a hint of furniture polish.

So far, so normal for a Catholic church.

Certainly nothing to suggest the presence of hidden Templar tombs.

The organ music stopped and the faint sound of conversation wafted down from on high, before the clacking of Camara's heels on stone steps and the peal of the organ began once more.

As she emerged back into the nave, Camara held up a ring of keys and beckoned Martin to join her.

They walked out to the side of the altar into a modern corridor, clearly added at a later stage for practical reasons, and could talk again once the sound of the organ was muted by the thick walls of the original church.

"The stairs to the crypt are back here," Camara explained. "The organ master said we could investigate on our own. He wants to practice, not wander round in the cobwebs below. He said the church once used the crypt for storage, but there was storm damage, so they locked it off a while back. With funds dwindling, and a focus on the needs of the modern church, it rarely gets any attention."

They walked through the corridor, passing meeting rooms before angling back to the older part of the church. At the very end, there was a small wooden door labelled *Entrée interdite*. No entry.

Camara tried several of the keys and finally unlocked the door with one of them. She pushed it open.

It was dark inside and the scent on the air changed from the incense of the church to a mustier, damp smell with a hint of wet stone.

Camara reached inside and switched on the light.

Metal stairs wound down through a circular well. While it began with modern bricks, there were enormous stone blocks further down, proving this section was much older than the area above.

Camara turned and raised an eyebrow. "What do you think?"

Martin frowned. Surely it was obvious. "We must go and see what lies down there. But you don't have to come with me if you don't want to."

Martin appreciated that Camara's last experience with the Catholic Church was as a possible sacrifice for an ultra-religious sect of monks who spent their lives protecting the location of the Garden of Eden. It was understandable if she didn't fancy the darkness of the crypt below.

"Of course I'm coming," she said with a grin.

"Besides, there are sometimes interesting lichen on these old tombs, and who can resist a *Caloplaca flavocitrina* in situ?"

She led the way down the spiral staircase, dainty in her heels and seemingly unaware of the dust motes that floated in the air and settled on her stylish suit. Camara was just as at home in the rarefied atmosphere of the Bibliothèque Nationale as she was investigating ancient plants in the field, so perhaps this place was nothing out of the ordinary. Martin considered that she might make an excellent ARKANE agent if she ever decided to change careers.

As they descended the stairs, it grew colder and the smell of wet stone intensified. They finally reached the bottom to find a crypt with a low ceiling lit by a single, bare bulb activated by the switch above. The weak light did not reach the edges of the space, but it was enough to illuminate the detritus within.

The crypt had clearly been used as a dumping ground, and the stale air reeked of rot and decay. Remnants of broken chairs and wooden pews were piled high next to bulging boxes of dusty paperwork. An old lawnmower surrounded by frayed bell-ringing ropes leaned against a pile of kneeling cushions with faded biblical scenes. There were even broken pieces of ancient tombstones brought down from the garden above. All of it lay in an inch of water that covered the flagstones beneath.

As he looked around at the discarded junk and debris, Martin began to have serious doubts this trip was worth the time.

Camara pulled out her phone and turned on its flashlight, holding it up to illuminate the shadows.

"Look, back there. Is that the edge of another door?"

Without waiting for Martin's response, she strode across the wet floor. Water splashed up her heels and stained the hem of her trouser suit but she walked on, oblivious. Martin followed, the chill of the dank water seeping into his shoes as he squelched behind.

Camara navigated around the reeking piles of rubbish and stopped in front of what was indeed another door above a raised threshold that kept it away from the flood.

Together, they shifted the boxes of old hymn books and discarded candle ends to one side and cleared a path to it.

Camara lifted her phone higher to bathe the door in the powerful light. "*Merveilleux.* It is magnificent."

The door was clearly ancient, constructed from a single tree trunk with knots and whorls weathered with age, and covered with a dark patina. There were indistinct letters carved into it and marks that might have been runes or protective talismans, but they were scuffed and scarred over, as if someone had tried to erase their meaning.

There were heavy metal hinges on one side of the door and, on the other, seven huge padlocks linked with an enormous chain covered in sharp spikes. The metal was rust-covered and oxidized, splintered and sharp, pitted by time.

Martin tilted his head to one side as he assessed the configuration of the chain and the angles of the padlocks, calculating the possible rust damage and how brittle the metal might be. He leaned forward and pressed a particularly rusty link of the chain with one delicate finger, testing its strength.

He frowned as he pulled a handkerchief from his pocket and wiped off the metallic residue. "There is a chance — a slim one — that we can break this chain and enter whatever lies beyond."

Camara nodded. "Then you and I will try it, *mon ami*. Since we are here and it's clear no one cares for this place. Paris is littered with secrets. Perhaps we will discover a new one together."

Martin looked around the crypt for something he could use as a lever to pry the chain from the door. Everything came down to numbers in the end and a skilled mathematician with a lever could move the world, as Archimedes himself knew.

After examining the rubbish pile, Martin picked out a wedge-shaped block of broken tombstone along with a heavy chunk of stone that fit in his hand and carried them over to the door.

Camara stood back as he placed the wedge in a particular spot behind the chain, adjusting it until it was just right.

Martin lifted the stone and smashed it down.

A dull metallic clang echoed in the crypt, and the chain inched away from the door.

As the noise faded into silence, Martin and Camara stood listening for footsteps, expecting someone to rush down and stop them.

But the faint strains of the organ could still be heard from high above, the organ master concentrating on notes rising to heaven, not those from the depths beneath.

Martin raised his makeshift hammer once more and pounded it down.

This time, the chain splintered and split. The rust fractured into red flakes that dropped down to stain the stagnant water beneath.

Martin used his elbow to break the rest of the links away, then pushed the door gently.

It didn't budge, so he leaned his weight against it.

The door creaked open to reveal more stone steps leading down into darkness — but this darkness had a different feel than that of the crypt.

The air was still, as if it hadn't been disturbed for generations, and it had the metallic tang of rust — or blood. Martin couldn't help but think of the torture chambers where Templar Knights had suffered their ultimate fate so long ago.

"*En avant,* Martin," Camara said, her voice almost a whisper, as if she did not want to disturb whatever lay below.

There was no light switch, no sign of anything modern, so they used their phone flashlights to illuminate the way.

Martin entered first, stepping carefully down onto the wet stone steps as he descended. As he looked back to make sure Camara was okay, he noticed that the thick walls on either side of the door were raked with deep gouges, as if something ancient had tried to claw its way out.

The stairwell spiralled down much further than Martin expected. The only sounds were their footsteps and the occasional drip of water onto stone.

He brushed away cobwebs, allowing the scuttling spiders to escape to the shadows. Some were bulbous and fat, gorging on whatever creatures writhed out of the spaces between the stones. Other arachnids were tiny and swift, freezing in the light as he passed. Some might have turned back and left this place to its denizens of the dark, but whenever

Martin checked with Camara, she urged him on, her eyes bright with curiosity in the glare of the flashlight.

After what seemed like an age, the stairs levelled out in front of a Gothic archway with Latin text carved on either side of its highest point.

Requiescant donec opus sit.

"Let them rest until needed," Camara translated, her tone a little puzzled. "That's unusual. I would have expected something more religious."

They walked under the arch and into the vault beyond.

It was sparse and plain, with none of the trappings that might be expected in a tomb. No carvings on the walls, no altar. In fact, it didn't feel like a tomb at all, and Martin had been in enough of them to know. The air felt expectant, as if the vault had been suspended in time for nearly a thousand years.

There were six sarcophagi placed equidistant on the flagstones around the vault.

Martin approached the nearest one and examined the lid. It was carved with a knight laid to rest, his sword held against his chest where the huge cross of his Templar tunic could be seen beneath.

Camara looked up at Martin. "The lid doesn't look heavy. We could perhaps move it together."

Martin felt a spark of curiosity within, along with

an atavistic dread that chilled his spine. His years with ARKANE had proved that there were things in this world better left undisturbed — but the mystery sparked by the mistakenly scanned document could only be solved by looking inside one of the sarcophagi.

He reached for the edge of the lid and tested its weight.

It shifted a little.

Martin walked to the end of the sarcophagus, and Camara joined him by the head of the knight.

Together, they lifted the lid and pushed it a few inches, opening a gap into the darkness within.

The scent of sandalwood and spices rose from the tomb, reminiscent of the winding streets of the souk in Jerusalem where pilgrims walked back when these knights had ridden to glory on crusade.

It was not the smell of the long dead.

Camara held up her phone with a shaking hand, and as the light skittered over what lay within, she gasped.

As the sound echoed around the vault, Martin's mind teemed with questions. For a moment, he wished he were back in front of his screens in a tiny closet in the Vatican and not facing what he suspected lay in front of them.

He looked down into the knight's face.

The man was maybe mid-forties, the skin around his eyes wrinkled from laughter and toil in the sun. A puckered scar curled out of a close-cropped beard around his strong jawline, evidence of past battles. The knight wore a chain mail hood, and the pommel of his sword was just visible in the shadows beneath the lid.

The knight's eyes were — thankfully — closed.

"How can this be?" Camara whispered.

"We have to see more." Martin placed his hands against the lid and pushed, alone now, as Camara stood frozen, holding her flashlight on the face of the knight.

The lid eased back further to reveal the knight's shoulders.

A thick leather strap bound him, secured with hooks to either side of a metal frame affixed to the stone with heavy rivets.

Martin's heart beat faster still.

He pushed again and the stone lid scraped across the edge of the sarcophagus to reveal the knight's torso.

There were more straps holding the knight, and he held his long sword against his chest.

But the red cross of the Templar tunic was marred by a spike through its centre. A heavy metal stake driven through the knight's heart.

There was only one explanation for such a creature. Martin did not want to speak the word out loud, but was it so strange to think that the Church hid such a secret?

The sacrament of transubstantiation taught that wine truly turned into blood, and the faithful drank it during Communion. Catholic cathedrals and chapels across the world contained body parts in holy vessels from saints whose martyred blood and flesh empowered the prayers of the faithful. Were these undead knights so unusual in such a religion?

Martin wondered what might happen if he pulled the stake out. Would this Soldier of God rise to defend the realm once more? And who might he consider the enemy in these modern times?

Camara raised her phone a little higher, and the light touched a book lying next to the knight. "Perhaps that will tell us more?"

Her voice trembled a little.

Martin reached in and grasped the book, careful not to touch the knight, just in case.

He drew it out and laid it on the lid of the sarcophagus. Its cover was thick brown leather marked by scars, like the hide of a creature well used to battle. Martin wasn't sure what kind of creature it came from, but he filed that question away for future consideration, along with the many others rising in his mind.

As Camara leaned closer, he carefully opened the book.

The pages within were handwritten in a barely legible scrawl, a legend in Latin with drawings of battles fought and plans of the medieval city of Paris. On its final pages there was a portrayal of this very vault, with the exhortation carved above a Gothic arch. The names of six knights were inscribed above the tombs. The one they had uncovered was Raymond de Payens.

Martin wondered what had led Raymond to his fate. His features were those of a man sleeping in peace, not those of one forced into the grave against his will. Had he chosen to become this undead creature?

A folded page was tucked into the book near the end, but Martin didn't want to open it down here. It could crumble with age and they would lose whatever knowledge lay within. But he also didn't want to take the book back to the Vatican or even reveal this location. The world had changed since medieval times and the Church was not so accepting of the truly supernatural.

Martin could use the temperature-controlled specialist labs at the ARKANE headquarters in London to research further — but perhaps he and Camara should just seal the book back up with its guardian and try to forget this place existed.

Camara looked around at the six tombs. "They are indeed resting until needed, but are they needed now? Should we wake them?"

Martin thought of the world above with its increasing environmental disasters, wars that took their toll while still more conflict threatened, the pandemic that kept people imprisoned by fear even years after it rose to kill millions. Perhaps these knights were needed more than ever, but Martin couldn't see how their ancient skills, whatever they might be, could help in a world of modern threats. They would be curiosities, or more likely imprisoned, interrogated, and tortured as their fellow Templars had been centuries ago.

He shook his head. "We may need them someday, but for now, let them continue to rest." He tapped the cover of the book. "I'll take this back to London. Perhaps there are answers within."

Camara nodded. "*Oui, bien sur.* It is better this way, at least for now."

As Martin pulled the lid closed, Camara's flashlight flickered over the knight's face. It gave an illusion of movement, a semblance of life, before the tomb shut him away once more, sealed back into darkness, ready to rise when needed.

Together, Martin and Camara slowly climbed back up the staircase to the crypt. They shifted the rotten piles of rubbish to more effectively hide the ancient door from view before ascending the last flight of stairs. Camara locked the crypt door once more, and Martin could only hope that others might heed its warning not to enter.

Back in the church, Camara walked up to the organ loft to hand over the keys. Martin heard her chatting with the organist in light tones, explaining away the cobwebs and dust on her clothes as nothing more than the detritus of the flooded crypt.

Martin stood in the nave and held the book close to his chest, eager to investigate its precious contents. A ray of sun arced through the stained glass window and touched the leather cover. It blistered and charred under the light, and the smell of smoke rose from its burning surface. Martin turned quickly, moving out of the sun into the shadows to examine the patch of scorched material. It was clearly made from the skin of a creature that burned in sunlight, and Martin shivered as he considered the nature of the knights left below. What else might he find in these medieval pages?

He took off his jacket and wrapped it around the book, turning it into a nondescript bundle of fabric, protecting the contents until he could get it back to the ARKANE labs to investigate.

Camara walked back down into the nave. Martin

joined her and together they emerged from the church onto Rue du Temple. Just another day in the city of lights.

Commuters still hurried past, coffee drinkers still sat at the café tables. Paris continued along the winding river of history, but Martin sensed something had shifted far beneath the streets.

They walked together along Rue du Temple, comfortable in their silence as they reached the banks of the River Seine and crossed the bridge to Île de la Cité. They navigated their way to the square in front of the cathedral of Notre-Dame, a symbol of the continued power of the Catholic Church and near to where the last Grandmaster of the Templars was burned to death by those he served.

Camara turned to Martin. "What will you do with the document in the scanned archives?"

"I'll decouple it from the papal bull and change the metadata, so it looks like some boring tax document. It will be lost amongst the millions of digital files. No one will find it."

Camara sighed. "And the book?"

"I'll take it back to the ARKANE vault in London for further study, and I'll tell Director Marietti what we found. He'll know what to do, and the knights can sleep on — at least for now."

Camara looked out across the Seine. "Do you

think there are more soldiers of God out there, hidden in buried vaults across the ancient Empire?"

Martin gave a half smile as the bells of Notre-Dame tolled another hour and the river of history flowed past. "Possibly. But let's hope they will rest until needed."

AUTHOR'S NOTE

Soldiers of God is a standalone story in the world of my ARKANE thrillers. You don't need to read the other books in the series to enjoy it.

Martin Klein, ARKANE's Head Librarian and Archivist, is a popular side character in the series and one I am particularly fond of. I love Bond movies and he's similar to 'Q'. Martin appears in almost all my ARKANE thrillers.

Professor Camara Mbaye featured in *Tree of Life*, ARKANE Thriller #11, and when Martin needed to go to Paris, I thought she might like to join him.

When I learned about the scanning of the Vatican Archives, I thought Martin might find a secret in there somewhere. I'm also fascinated by how artificial intelligence tools can augment human creativity and wondered how such a tool might help uncover knowledge once thought lost.

The papal bull, *Militia Dei*, Soldiers of God, is real. It was issued by Pope Eugene III in 1145 and granted the Templars the right to take tithes and burial fees and to bury their dead in their own cemeteries. The extra document is my invention. At least I think so…

There was a medieval Templar fortress in the Marais district of Paris. When the covered market, Carreau du Temple, was undergoing renovations in 2007, the investigators found the remains of a Templar cemetery. Who knows what lies beneath?

* * *

If you'd like more action adventure stories with an edge of religious history and a touch of the supernatural, check out my ARKANE thrillers, starting with *Stone of Fire*.

Related links

"Artificial Intelligence is Cracking Open the Vatican's Secret Archives," *The Atlantic*, 30 April 2018 — www.theatlantic.com/technology/archive/2018/04/vatican-secret-archives-artificial-intelligence/559205/

Vatican Library Digital Archives — digi.vatlib.it

"The Secret Seat of the Knights Templar," BBC Travel, 25 July 2019 — www.bbc.co.uk/travel/article/20190724-the-knights-templars-mightiest-stronghold

BLOOD, SWEAT, AND FLAME

IT'S STILL DARK WHEN I cycle into the court-yard outside the glassblowing hot shop and lean my bike against the side of the industrial warehouse, its chimneys reaching toward the brightening sky. My breath frosts in the air, a sign that autumn is waning and winter creeps ever closer.

The harsh caw of a crow echoes from the copse of trees that shield the warehouse from the main road. A ray of dawn turns the brick wall to the colour of crushed cochineal, a red so dark it's almost black. The smell of rot and decay drifts on the air from the adjacent mushroom farm. I imagine the creeping threads of mycelium reaching blindly under the earth, curling around dead creatures, squirming their way toward the light.

I take off my threadbare gloves and rub my hands together to warm them before digging out the keys from my pack. There are a few hours before my shift officially starts, time enough to work on another tiny piece of my sculpture.

Production glass blowing pays the bills, but every tray load of wine glasses or tourist baubles gives me another chance to work overtime on my creation. Artisans can work here for an hourly rate, but the owner doesn't notice, or perhaps doesn't care, that I take my turn before the production day even starts. As long as the furnaces are blasting and ready for other workers when the clock ticks over nine, I'm left alone.

I unlock the heavy wooden door and stand for a moment in the darkness of the corridor. The cabinet looms before me, the shapes within indistinct, but I know every inch by heart.

A decade of trophies for original glass blown sculptures.

All with his name on.

I turn on the light and consider the evidence of his triumph. The carefully etched letters are a blur to me now, and they will probably worsen this winter. A year at the most, the optician said, when I last scraped up the money to visit. Avoid bright light, she said, oblivious to the burning heart of the furnace I stand before every day. It transforms base sand to ethereal glass even as it mutates me, cell by cell.

I pass by and head to the hot shop entrance, the trophy cabinet looming behind me, like the demanding presence of a jealous god. I grab my leather apron from the locker and tie it over my jeans, the faded denim blistered with burn holes from dripping molten glass, a patchwork over my scarred skin. Every culture has its fire deity, and the furnace demands its sacrifice. Fire for blood.

Perhaps I have not given enough.

As I bang the locker door shut, a puff of air ruffles the edges of the paper announcements on the notice board. Adverts for assistants, second-hand tools for sale, and the sculpture contest guidelines displayed prominently in the centre. The deadline for entry creeps closer every day.

I turn on the bright overhead lights of the warehouse. Even though I long for the heat of the furnace, I appreciate these moments of cold solitude. The smell of metal mingled with beeswax. A lingering scent of ash from burned newspaper and smoke from flaming cork pads.

The smell of home.

It might as well be, since I spend most of my time here. I can barely stand to eat or sleep in my tiny council flat. The thin walls fail to mask the noise of the family next door, laughing and fighting, the constant chatter of a shared life.

I turn on the furnaces, readying the hot shop for the production workers and artisans who will arrive all too soon. I strip off my outer layers as the temperature rises and soon, I'm sweating in my T-shirt, my roughly cropped grey hair bound back in a marigold cotton scarf, dug out of lost property years back and tattered with repeated washing.

Some call us the truckers of the art world, sweaty,

smelly, physical laborers in the heat and grime of the hot shop. Those precious writers who craft words with their minds in hushed libraries can never understand us. They remain safe in their pristine sanctuary while I sculpt with light, my scars evidence of devotion to the muse of flame.

Sunlight streams through the high windows, illuminating my test pieces of glass lined up along one frame. I need a range of colours for my final sculpture, and I have yet to find the perfect shade of crimson for its heart. I have shards of opal, coral, and tornado red, spun in frit from colour bars. I've experimented with ruby, fuchsia, and saffron transparents, and I've even tried adding copper foil.

But something is missing.

Every day I experiment with new combinations, but the dancing flame eludes me.

The main furnace is at full strength now. Two thousand degrees Fahrenheit. Hotter than a cremation incinerator and certainly more than enough to burn a body down to its elemental parts. It's how I want to go when it's my time. A final union of flesh and flame.

I open the glory hole and stare into the heart of the fire, safety glasses dangling at my side. My heart beats faster. The rush of light fills my vision and I can almost feel it burn away another tiny speck of who I am in exchange for another day of creation. Djinns dance in the flame, a promise of transformation, and I can't help but smile. They don't always appear, but when they do, the glass transfigures for me. There is no true art without pain, so I take my tiny dose every day.

Or perhaps it's just how I feed the firebug in my soul.

With one last glance into the blaze, I put on my safety glasses and the vision fades as the light dims.

I gather molten glass with my blowpipe, legs braced apart, back muscles stiff with the initial lift of the day. The first puff of air into the hollow tube is always a relief, as if I hold my breath when I'm away from the hot shop, unwilling to exhale completely until I can bring life to a new piece.

I flash the glass in the glory hole, resting the pole on the yoke as the temperature heats it once more. A dance of motion and heat, of melting and shaping and cooling as the figure takes shape.

It is the fifth time I've tried this central aspect of the sculpture, and I can see the finished piece in my mind. A bird rising from a twisted prone figure in shades of blood and fire, copper and gold, surrounded by tongues of flame.

But the challenge of art is never the idea, only the execution.

I use a rubber tube attached to the end of the hollow pipe to puff a little more air into the globe, spinning the rod over the bench as I cradle it with a wet pad. Glasswork is easier with an assistant, but I've learned to hack the process over years working alone. I can even pull cane solo with an anchor point on the wall.

Steam rises and sweat beads on my brow. The minutes melt away as I lean into the magic of creation.

The sound of my breath.

The roar of the furnace.

The whoosh of the blowtorch as I shape the figure, curving the glass under my *tagliol* knife.

The door bangs, and a waft of cold air enters the hot shop.

I lose my concentration and the torch flares in my hand, the shape of the emerging phoenix muddling to a blob.

"Early again?" Jeremy says the same words in the same tone every morning.

"Lots to do." My reply is as light as ever.

Jeremy's award-winning pieces are technically brilliant, I acknowledge that. But he has the time and money to focus on his craft with no need for income from production glass or other menial work. He is a gentleman glassblower, with some hidden way of turning life into money with no seeming effort.

He occasionally teaches at the art college — not the beginner classes, mind you. Only the intricate and complicated later stages of glassblowing. Jeremy does not tolerate amateurs.

He lives with his family on the other side of town in a large house passed down by his grandfather. I attended one of his victory parties a few years back when he still considered me worth inviting. The chandeliers were antique Venetian, the wine glasses individually hand crafted, and his artworks perched like glorious birds of paradise all over the house.

His winning sculpture that year sat on a mahogany table, pride of place in what they called the drawing room. A stark piece in black and clear glass, a man's torso with the figure of a child nestled within.

His only son. His muse. Each of his winning pieces has featured some aspect of their relationship. The play of light and dark, the love of a father for his son.

I exhale sharply into my blowpipe, expelling withheld words into glass.

Jeremy goes to his station and begins his routine, selecting his preferred colour bars.

The tap of the hammer.

The squeak of hinges on his glory hole.

The puff of his first breath.

I can't help but imagine what he might create this time. I know I should keep my gaze in my own lane, but with so little time left, it's hard not to think about it.

I pour some water on the jack point and tap the punty. The glass breaks at its weakest point and my ruined piece drops into the metal bucket. The clink of shattering glass is a sound glassblowers know well. Jeremy doesn't even look up.

I gather molten glass once more, this time for the first production of the day, and as I walk back to my bench, I glance over at his.

Pistachio and olive green colour bars. Turquoise and even some blue aventurine, the cobalt inclusions creating silvery metallic sparkles. He has artistic range, that's for sure, and every year, Jeremy has surprised the judges by pushing the boundaries of his technical ability.

He keeps his creation process hidden and even has a personal annealer in the corner of the warehouse. His glass cools away from the mass production boxes where I have to edge my art into corners when there is space. I have glimpsed some of his pieces, all over-sized with organic curves, but I can't picture what they might become.

The door bangs again and a young man walks in, his lanky frame erect with the confident swagger of the privileged. His dark hair is close cropped, his skin has the burnished glow of youth and the evidence of a late holiday in the sun. His profile matches his father's but without the wrinkles and burn marks from years in front of a hot furnace.

"Come in, Isaac."

Jeremy beckons him over. His son pulls out his phone to check a message before sauntering over to the bench.

Isaac glances at me as he walks by, and I see a glimmer of curiosity as his gaze slides towards the open door of the glory hole. Perhaps there is a firebug in him waiting to ignite.

I still remember my first time in the hot shop, the roar and heat of the furnace and smoke billowing from wet pads applied to burning glass. A dangerous art, for sure, but at least here, I make my own scars. Pain has a different quality if you choose it.

"Let's start with something simple."

I tune out Jeremy's words and Isaac's grunted replies as I shift into the rhythm of repetitive production.

Gather. Turn. Blow. Shape. Cool.

I can do this with my eyes closed. Perhaps I will need to do it that way soon enough.

The hours pass and the conversation behind me becomes heated. The sound of smashing glass happens too often to be ignored.

Isaac is not a willing student, or at least not inclined to learn from his father. I hear frustration in Jeremy's voice, a desire to share genuine passion with his son. Yet somehow, he can't get through.

A crash of glass against metal.

"That's enough." Jeremy bites out his words. "I don't have time for this. Go help Cass. She might even teach you a thing or two. At least you'll only break cheap production glass."

His words dismiss my years of experience, and the heavy workload that pays the bills. I ignore them, bracing my shoulders as I flash glass in the glory hole, leaning toward the dry heat, relishing the sweat on my skin. I sit down at the bench again and turn the pipe, keeping the glass moving, shaping it with callipers.

Hesitant footsteps approach on the concrete behind me and I feel his gaze on my back. I turn my head, sharp words on the tip of my tongue ready to cut him down and send him back to his father.

But Isaac's gaze is fixed on the turning glass in my hands, reflected sparks from the furnace leaping in his eyes. Perhaps we both compare ourselves to the master craftsman and find ourselves wanting.

I swallow my cutting words as he walks to the side of my bench.

"What are you making?"

"A batch of wine glasses for a catering company." I nod toward the annealer where the finished glasses cool slowly. "They all have to be exactly the same."

Isaac picks up a pair of shears. "I've used these at school. We made some simple vessels. I know it's not much but…"

His words trail off and I see myself years ago. The art of glassblowing is ancient, passed down from master to apprentice for thousands of years. Perhaps Isaac just needs the right teacher.

"Can you blow as I turn?"

He nods and bites his lip. "Yes, I've done that before."

"Okay, just let me finish this one."

Isaac grabs two heavy gloves. "I can put it in the annealer if you like."

I look down at the almost finished piece and weigh up the risk. More smashed glass, more wasted time. But if he can be of use, we might even finish early.

He crouches down, gloves ready, his gaze fixed intently on the turning glass. His phone buzzes in his pocket, but he doesn't seem to notice. He holds his breath in concentration.

"Ready?"

He nods.

I dribble water on the jack point, then tap the pipe with my callipers.

The finished wine glass drops onto his gloves. He holds it like a precious chalice, his grip gentle but firm.

I walk ahead of him to the annealer and open the door, half-expecting a crash behind me. But he places the glass gently inside next to the others with no mishap.

As I close the door, his breath comes fast, his cheeks are flushed, his eyes bright with enthusiasm. Perhaps he might be useful after all.

"Let's do another."

We work in silence on the next glass, and the next. He shows no sign of tiring or boredom and we both ignore Jeremy working behind us, even though I sense the intensity of his gaze now and then.

Eventually he stalks across the floor and stands over us, looming like a professor about to give a lecture. My back muscles tense and I'm acutely aware of the blue-collar vessel at the end of my turning pole. No doubt Jeremy hasn't made something so basic for decades.

"Thanks, Cass. I hope he hasn't been any trouble."

"Quite the opposite. After all, we're only working on cheap production glass."

There's a flicker of annoyance in his eyes and his mouth tightens a little at my retort. He looks at his son.

"I'm heading off now. Want a lift home?"

Isaac glances up from where he kneels at the end of the pipe. A new supplicant to an ancient art.

"No, I'll head back later." He looks at me. "If that's okay with you, Cass?"

"Of course."

Jeremy exhales heavily. "I'll see you at home later."

The door bangs on his way out and the atmosphere in the hot shop lifts. There is no judgment in the flame and Isaac blossoms once his father has gone.

We pull ahead of my usual schedule, and I let him have a go at gathering and turning a piece. As he flashes the bulb, he pushes too hard on the yoke.

The glass smashes against the side of the furnace, tinkling onto the concrete.

"I'm sorry, I'm so clumsy." He places the punty to one side and bends to sweep up the glass, dumping it in the metal bucket.

"It's the sound of learning. A totally normal part of glasswork."

He smiles up at me, relief in his eyes.

We get back to it and within a few tries, he manages to make a plain wine glass. It's not perfect, but it's functional and it's more than he has ever made with his father. He places it in the annealer with a smile of pride on his lips.

As we walk back to the furnace together, his phone buzzes in his pocket.

He pulls it out, reads the text, shakes his head with a sigh. "Dad."

Isaac bashes out a reply, his thumbs moving quickly. "He'll get mad if he knows I'm still here with you. I'll say I'm with a friend who lives nearby." He glances up. "Is it okay if I stay a little longer? Maybe you can show me how to make something else?"

I don't have the time, but his expectant gaze is that of a true apprentice.

I nod. "Of course."

He finishes the text and smiles up at me, his attention diverted for a split second.

The phone slips out of his hand, landing in the metal bucket of broken glass shards by the side of the furnace.

He reaches down before I can stop him.

His palm catches on a sharp edge, and he jerks away, clutching his hand.

Blood drips from between his fingers down onto the shards of glass, catching the light from the furnace.

Ruby. Carnelian. A hint of Emperor purple.

The missing shade.

A second stretches out, a twisted glass cane of possible futures.

With one hand I reach for a thick pad and with the other, I pick up the *tagliol* knife.

*   *   *

A month later, I stand in front of the trophy cabinet. My name is etched on the copperplate where it belongs, even though I can hardly make out the words now.

The judges noted my particular use of colour, the intensity of red at the heart of the phoenix, giving its life to the fire as it rises from ash into new life.

As I grab my leather apron from the locker, the air ruffles the edges of a Missing notice. The beloved son of a prominent glass artist gone before his time.

AUTHOR'S NOTE

During the pandemic lockdowns, many of us escaped into binge-watching Netflix. I discovered the world of glassblowing and the intensity of the hot shop through *Blown Away*, a reality show based around glass art. The characters of the first series and the danger inherent in flames, metal, and molten glass inspired this story.

SINS OF TREACHERY

THE PRIEST INTONED THE Canticle Benedictus, his breath freezing in the air as the solid oak casket was lowered into the hardened ground. Simon bent to pick up a handful of damp earth to throw on the coffin, holding the grainy soil in his palm. He focused on the ground, taking a moment to breathe through the wave of grief.

A thud of earth on wood.

Simon looked up quickly as someone else performed the family honour for the dead. When he saw who it was, the forgotten soil spilled from his hand.

Gest, his errant twin, had finally returned, but only after the death of the man who raised them.

"Grant this mercy, O Lord, we beseech Thee, to Thy servant departed, that he may not receive in punishment the requital of his deeds who in desire did keep Thy will…"

As the priest said the final prayers, Gest smiled across the grave, his pale hazel eyes and high cheekbones a perfect mirror of Simon's own, yet somehow an air of superiority and entitlement set him apart.

His black pea-coat was perfectly tailored, and Simon was suddenly aware of his own ill-fitting suit borrowed for the occasion. At a superficial level, they were identical twins, but Simon had always felt like a pale imitation, a watery reflection of his brother's bright colour. Jealousy rekindled within him, a remnant of childhood rivalry. Try as he might, Simon had never been able to take the place of the favoured twin with his grandfather, despite his labour in the pursuit of the Great Work.

"May his soul, and the souls of all the faithful departed, through the mercy of God, rest in peace. Amen."

The gathered crowd mumbled Amen from bowed heads and began to move away from the grave. Simon shook hands and nodded appropriately as people spoke kindly to him of his grandfather. But his eyes kept straying to Gest, who stood silently by the grave, his tightly wound energy repelling any who thought to approach him. Finally, when the last of the mourners left, Simon walked to his brother's side. They stood together looking into the pit, a reminder of where all must finally rest.

"Why now?" Simon asked, his voice clipped, almost breaking.

"He sent me a letter asking me to come a few weeks' back. Said he had something for me, something you were unwilling to take to its conclusion." Gest turned, his eyes as cold as the grave. "Where is it?"

He put his hand on Simon's arm, fingers gripping tight. Memories of youth flooded back and Simon remembered their games, how his bruises and broken bones were always blamed on clumsiness, how Gest was praised for caring so much for his brother – the weaker twin, the slower twin, the twin less blessed. That hand was still able to crush and dominate.

Simon flinched, as the years peeled away. "It's back at the house."

* * *

The mansion would have been opulent once, but its grandeur had faded through many years of neglect. Gest strode ahead into the dark entrance hall, quick steps taking him into dusty rooms the brothers had run through together as children, hiding amongst the towering bookcases, their palaces of imagination.

"It really hasn't changed much." He ran a finger along the grimy mantelpiece. "Seriously Si, how have you managed to live in this gloomy place for so long?"

Simon watched his brother's mercurial movements, his confident stride. He had always been the saturnine twin, the dark opposite to Gest's golden sun.

"I've been helping Grandfather. You know how much his research meant to him, and now to me."

Gest laughed, and Simon felt his years of intellectual pursuit dismissed in a heartbeat.

He had heard rumours of how Gest had spent the last twelve years, his string of beautiful women and exotic travels funded by the wealth they were both supposed to inherit, his expensive tastes paid for by ever-dwindling funds. Simon knew that lust had also ruled his grandfather's early life, but the old man had wanted something different as he aged, searching for power and fulfilment beyond material things. Simon desired influence far beyond his brother's petty pleasures, but there had been days when he had longed to lose himself in an orgy of flesh.

Gest shrugged. "How you live your life is your own choice. But I want what he promised me, then I'll leave you alone in this melancholic place."

"His gift is in the lab. It's been extended since you were last here." Simon walked ahead through the dilapidated hallway to a metal door and pushed it open. "This way."

The neglected main house was in stark contrast to the gleaming laboratory, secretly constructed, where no one would have suspected that Simon and his grandfather continued to pursue the Great Work of the alchemists. Cutting edge science mingled with the occult, chemical formulas jostling for position with the symbols of medieval hermetics.

Gest walked through the lab, glancing from side to side with little interest. He idly picked up a round-bottomed flask and swirled the ruby liquid within.

"Careful with that." Simon snatched the flask away and placed it carefully back onto its stand.

Gest moved around the end of the bench. "That's his book, isn't it?"

Simon turned to see Gest fingering his grand-father's most precious tome, open to a page of intricately detailed symbols inscribed with spidery handwriting around the edge.

"It's mine now. He gave it to me." Simon thought back to the night when he had ripped the book from his grandfather's embrace. The old man begged to hold it once more, his arms outstretched in need, covered with tattoos of words he had never explained. His eyes were shadowed with dread as he reached for it, filled with sinister memories the man couldn't help but relive, but would never speak of aloud. Simon had thrust the vodka bottle at him, his grandfather's addiction the only way to quiet the old man, while he delved ever deeper into the esoteric mysteries within.

Simon watched anxiously as Gest picked up the book, desperate to tear it from his brother's irreverent hands. Its cover was a patchwork of different coloured leather, sewn with cords and pulled tight like scars on a chequered board of human skin. The spine and pages were edged with gold, a work of art even without the precious words inside.

Turning away as if he cared nothing for the book, Simon walked to a large print on the wall. Intricately woven symbols of the planets, astrological signs and their alchemical metals were etched in pitch black upon a white background. The iron of Mars, the god of war, and Mercury's quicksilver, ruling planet of the twins of Gemini. He touched one side of the print and it swung from the wall to reveal a safe.

"So that's where the old bastard hid his treasure." Gest dropped the book with a thump onto the bench.

Simon reached into the safe, took a heavy manila envelope out, and handed it to his brother. "Grandfather always said this was for you, and that I wasn't to open it."

It had clearly been opened.

Gest arched one perfectly groomed eyebrow and Simon shrugged. "I didn't seriously believe you would come back for it."

Gest pulled the papers out of the envelope and frowned as he studied the pages, a combination of handwritten diary entries scrawled with notes and modern GPS printouts. He looked up with a question in his eyes.

Simon smiled with perverse pleasure at his brother's ignorance. "It's a map, or a series of them. Grandfather told me about it after his first heart attack. He pleaded with me to follow the directions, to take the path he always wanted to. He spent most of his life trying to work out the symbols in the book, and towards the end, he said he had finally discovered the key. But he was on so much morphine by then, I dismissed his ranting. That must have been when he sent the letter to you."

Gest spread the pages out on a worktop, scanning them quickly. "These look authentic, Si, and I'm sure you're aware of the state of the bank accounts. We need this or we're both finished."

"Even if it takes everything we have left?" Simon looked around at his beloved lab, wondering if the risk was worth it even as a desire rose within him to discover what lay at the end of the map.

Gest grinned, his eyes sparkling with a lust for adventure. "Even if it takes every cent. We'll get it back a thousand-fold. Remember Grandfather's stories, the ones he told us as boys by the fire as the wind howled outside. Diamonds and precious stones and gems without name, just waiting for us to pull them from the ice. Now we have the map to show us the way."

Gest embraced his brother, spinning him around the lab. Simon reluctantly gave into his merriment, smiling for the first time since his grandfather's death, finally understanding why the map had been left to his headstrong, reckless twin.

* * *

Two months later

Simon shook his head as he thought back to that moment in the lab, the beginning of this trip to the frozen wastelands of the far north.

The map had indicated a little-known stratum of caves within the Arctic Circle, but their ship could carry them no further and now they had to take dog sleds for the final section of the journey inland.

The expedition had drained the last of the bank loans that Gest secured against the mansion and the lab, and Simon cursed his own weakness at letting his brother mortgage his life's work. His jaw ached from days of clenching it; each thunk of ice crunching on the side of the hull reminded him of the miles of frozen water between them and civilisation.

There was no going back.

The specialist team finished the last checks of the equipment they needed to carry inland, and Simon stood on the ice watching as the handlers brought the sled dog teams out from the ship. The Siberian huskies and Alaskan malamutes leapt about yelping, shaking their shaggy fur, tongues hanging out as their hot breath frosted the air. They were reminiscent of wolves with sharp teeth and thick fur, animals suited to this cruel environment, ready to do battle with Nature.

"Cry havoc," Simon whispered, "and let slip the dogs of war."

He zipped up his fur-lined coat, his hand skimming the top pocket where his name was sewn in violet letters to help the crew tell the identical twins apart. As if he could be mistaken for his brother, Simon thought, as he watched Gest arguing with the expedition leader, making sure the man followed his instructions to the letter.

Since his brother's attention was elsewhere, Simon bent to check the position of the book within his pack. He had wrapped it in multiple protective and waterproof layers, but he still felt a need to reaffirm its safety.

As he placed his hand upon it, a curious warmth emanated from within, a pulse that seemed to quicken as the book moved closer to its home. Simon looked up to see gusts of wind on the ice, swirling into figures like mutated angels as they reached for the book with misshapen hands. He blinked and they dissolved into eddies of chill air. Simon tightened the straps on his pack, pulling it closer to his body as the team readied to move out.

* * *

Later that day, the expedition leader called a halt as he and Gest checked their coordinates on the old paper map against the modern GPS. Simon peered around, squinting at the sun through his goggles, taking in their surroundings with a dawning sense of recognition. The shallow valley with a silhouette of icy hills around them matched one of the drawings in the book, crimson lines etched in a shaky hand that his grandfather had never been able to interpret.

With rising excitement, Simon stepped off his sled. He snapped on cross-country skis and headed towards the edge of the valley, using poles to spur himself onward. The barking and howling of dogs followed him and he heard Gest shout in alarm, but he wanted to be the first to confirm whether this was indeed the place in the drawing. He rushed ahead around a curve in the valley floor.

Before him, a precipice fell into a vast pit beneath a strange formation of ice cliffs reminiscent of a demon's head. A dank and foul-smelling waterfall crashed into the depths, the dark water a sharp contrast to the clear crystal they had found elsewhere. Stones the colour of iron encrusted with mould edged around the volcanic crevasse. Steam poured from the hole, filling the air with a hot stench like decaying flesh. Simon stood on the rim, part of him desperate to turn and run, and yet a dark sense called to the murky depths below as he gazed down into the tumbling waters.

Gest arrived on his skis, panting a little with the exertion of catching his brother, his face clouded with annoyance at being left behind.

"The map says that the caves are accessible from the waterfall," Gest said, as if he had found the location. "We're going down there. We're close, I can feel it."

The rest of the expedition team arrived and soon the crew were busy hammering in equipment and setting up abseiling gear.

Gest was impatient and, as soon as he could, he descended first with his head-lamp on, ignoring the expedition leader's request for initial safety checks. As he disappeared beneath the lip of the waterfall, Simon hurried his own preparation, quickly following Gest over the edge.

He glanced down, watching as his brother ducked under an overhang into a concealed cavern, unhooking his safety ropes in order to move more freely. Simon felt a pulse of excitement at finding the cave, a throbbing that seemed to vibrate through his pack from the book. Could this really be the place?

As he reached the cavern entrance, a low moan echoed from within, a deep sound of horror that was scarcely human, then retching and coughing.

Simon unhooked his harness and hurried down the rocky corridor into the cavern, blue light filtering down as the walls turned to ice away from the heat of the waterfall. As his head lamp flickered and reflected off the surface, Simon caught a glimpse of his own face as if in a mirror, startling him with the resemblance to his twin. He rounded a corner to find Gest bent double as he threw up the remains of his meagre breakfast, the smell of vomit permeating the chill of the cave. Gest pointed and Simon turned slowly, his head lamp illuminating what his brother had seen.

A cylindrical block of ice bisected the cavern. There were bodies inside, split open, hacked apart, frozen limbs protruding in bulges. Simon walked around it, breathing deeply, swallowing down the bile that filled his throat.

One man was split from chin to groin, his entrails dragged from his body, his heart cut from his chest, mutilated intestines frozen into a tableau of agony. Another figure lay face down, his head crushed, his back torn open by claws that rent his spine, exposing bones through ragged flesh flayed from his body. Who – or what – had done this?

Gest leaned against the wall, his face pale. He took a swig of water to rinse his mouth and then spat it out onto the floor of the cave, where it swiftly froze. "What do you think happened to them?"

Simon pointed at one of the dead, his head twisted around to face the back of his body, eyes frozen open. The man's clothes were the style and fabric of an earlier generation. "Whatever it was, it happened a long time ago."

Gest took a deep breath. "Do you think Grandfather knew of this?"

Simon heard judgment in his brother's voice, but he only felt a growing kinship with his grandfather's quest.

He swung off his pack and removed the book of multi-hued leather. It seemed to pulse in his hands as Simon flicked through the pages looking for the handwritten notes he had glimpsed once and now perhaps began to understand. He found them and smoothed the page open.

It showed a rough map of the north with the label Hyperborea inscribed in blood and twin lightning bolts scrawled at the bottom. A demon squatted in the middle of the land mass, a creature of primal myth, six wings beating against the cold north wind.

His grandfather had never been able to explain what it meant but now Simon felt a heat rise from the book, a throb of latent power. Light emanated from it and Simon's vision flashed. He saw the cave floor awash with blood, bodies hacked apart as a team of explorers died at the hands of a possessed madman who fled alone with the book, claiming its power.

Gest shone his torch away from the corpses towards the back of the cave, where light reflected in sparkling facets of brilliant colour.

"Radio above," he said, no longer focused on the wretched forms of the dead, but on the potential riches beyond. "Tell them to wait while we investigate further. We mustn't let anyone else see this."

The visions of violence dissipated with Gest's interruption and Simon found himself obeying in a daze. He walked to the mouth of the cavern and radioed that all was fine, and they would report again in another hour. As he walked back through the cave of the dead, Simon tucked the book into his inner clothing, close to his heart, relishing the strength that he drew from its growing potency, his heartbeat synchronising with its strange pulse.

As he reached the inner chamber, Gest turned, his face illuminated by the flashlight, eyes aflame with desire for limitless wealth. "Look Si, these are diamonds. This is where I rebuild my fortune… Where *we* rebuild our fortune, brother. Together."

Simon nodded, moving closer to examine the gems embedded in the ice wall. Behind the shining stones, he could see a darker shadow in the shape of an altar.

He sensed that it was the true goal and his excitement soared as he realised that the Great Work could indeed be finished. He would return the book to its rightful place and claim the reward beyond temporal riches, leaving the jewels to the greed of his twin.

Simon reached for his pack and unhooked his pickaxe. He gripped the handle and hefted its weight, giving it a few swings to test the action.

"Careful with that," Gest said, his voice imperious.

At his brother's tone, Simon felt a sudden desire for great physical strength, a need to turn his body into hard, powerful muscle. He was sick of being considered the studious weakling, disgusted with himself for allowing his brother's dominance for so long.

He swung the axe heavily into the wall and a thud resounded through the chamber. Simon levered a chunk of the bejewelled ice to the floor where Gest broke it into smaller pieces with a hammer and chisel, picking out the shining gems. They soon removed their outer jackets, working up a sweat in the small cave with their labour. The pile of jewels grew larger, and Gest started to fill his rucksack.

With one giant swing, Simon broke through into an alcove carved by ancient human hands. He worked faster to hack away the remaining ice and revealed an altar of black stone carved with mysterious symbols. There was an indentation in the middle, and Simon instinctively knew that the book should be laid there.

Gest stood up to look more closely. "What is it? Do you think it's worth anything?"

Simon's rage erupted at his brother's disregard for the sacred. He turned in anger. Gest shrank back at his brother's expression, stretching out his hands in mock surrender.

"Okay, okay. Let's just pack up the gems and get out of here. The team can come down and dig out the rest, but these jewels, we keep for ourselves."

As Gest bent to fasten his pack, Simon reached into his jacket for the book. He unwrapped the precious tome, dark pleasure rising within him as he touched its outer skin. With reverence, he placed it on the altar within the boundaries of the indentation. It fit perfectly and Simon knelt before it, bending his head in veneration.

Behind him, Gest snorted in derision at his actions.

As Simon rose and turned in anger, the chamber trembled, as if giants shook their limbs to free themselves from the ice.

A hail of rock fell from the ceiling and the brothers covered their heads. A chunk knocked Simon over and he landed heavily on his side, his skull smacking against the ground. His vision darkened and then cleared again as he sat up and rubbed his head, pain lancing through him.

The altar had split down the centre of the rock beneath the book and icy vapour oozed out of the newly formed crack, dissipating into the air. Afraid that the book would be damaged, Simon reached for it, breathing in the tainted air as he did so. It smelled metallic and he tasted blood in his mouth, then his senses sharpened, and he heard a terrible howl pouring from the abyss below beneath the beating of demonic wings.

"We'd better hurry," Gest said, as if he couldn't hear the frenzied clamour or see the cloudy haze. "Clearly this cave isn't stable. We need to get the jewels out while we still can."

He forced another chunk of gemstone into his pack. It shone in the lamplight and Simon caught a glimpse of his brother's reflection.

Gest's handsome face turned into that of a hideous lizard and behind him, a curved scorpion's tail emerged from his ripped snowsuit. Simon fell back against the wall, watching as his twin's face morphed from the Gest he knew into a sinister visage of reptilian scales, forked tongue flickering in the air.

Something within him understood that this unholy demon was his brother's true nature revealed by the book. There was only one way he could stop it.

Simon surged forward, his strength amplified from within. He pushed his brother to the ground, raising the pickaxe once more.

As Gest screamed in terror, Simon brought the weapon down. He became the avenger, the destroyer, hacking relentlessly at his brother's body as words from the precious book of skin ran through his mind.

Simon's breath was ragged as he finally cleaved the head from the mutilated torso, the ice slippery with gore as what remained of Gest's body began to harden with ice crystals.

Another tremor rocked the cavern. There was

little time before it collapsed, concealing both riches and the murder within.

The two padded outer jackets lay side by side away from the bloody mess. Simon stood looking at them, thinking of the divergent lives that he and Gest had experienced. In that moment he saw a possible future, where earthly pleasure and power could be his as well as the Great Work fulfilled.

He removed his bloody top, chest exposed to the chill air, revealing a tattoo of an orb cupped within a bowl on top of an inverted cross. Simon tugged a fresh merino sweater from his pack, pulled it over his head and zipped Gest's jacket on over the top. He straightened his back, adopting his brother's proud posture, then he picked up the two heavy packs and headed for the waterfall. It was time to tell the crew that his brother Simon had perished within the cavern as it collapsed, despite his own desperate attempts at rescue.

Behind him, icy vapour rose from the altar, winding its way out of the ancient cavern into the world above.

AUTHOR'S NOTE

Sins of Treachery is one of three short stories originally written as part of an online competition, *The Descent*, run by Kobo, an online ebook and audiobook retailer, for the launch of Dan Brown's thriller *Inferno* in 2013.

The Descent was based on Dante's *Inferno* and the stories featured as the opening to a transmedia game that linked to special websites, using symbols, words, and numbers from the story as clues to the next step.

My brief was to write three interlinking stories using the symbolism of Dante's *Inferno*, grouped into the main categories of sin. I published the three stories together in a previous collection, *A Thousand Fiendish Angels*, but the 'buried' theme seemed particularly apt here so I wanted to also include this story.

As part of my research, I read a modern translation of Dante's *Inferno* and made notes on the text, writing down images and specific words to use in my stories that would echo the rings of Hell.

In *Sins of Treachery*, Simon whispers, "Cry havoc,

and let slip the dogs of war," spoken by Anthony after the murder of Julius Caesar in Shakespeare's play of the same name. The traitors who led that insurrection are in the deepest circle of Inferno, in the mouth of Satan himself.

The Arctic location echoes Dante's Hell, which is encased in ice, and the entrance is through a 'precipice of dark-tinted water'. The tortured, distorted bodies of the men in the ice pillar reflect the terrible wounds of the treacherous and the fraudulent, some torn apart and disembowelled by demons for eternity.

Occult and mythological symbols were used to evoke the atmosphere of *Inferno* and also to lead to further clues within the original *Descent* game. In *Sins of Treachery*, symbols of the planets, astrological signs and their alchemical metals are shown on the safe door, featuring the iron of Mars, the god of war, and Mercury's quicksilver, ruling planet of the twins of Gemini.

The names of the characters also resonate with *Inferno*. Simon Magus is punished in the Eighth circle of Hell for Fraud, and Gestas was the impenitent thief crucified alongside Jesus, greedy for more.

THE DARK QUEEN

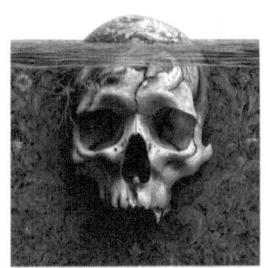

"COME ON, MARK." I SMILE up at him with a hint of flirtation. "Just one more dive. I won't be long."

Mark, the Dive Crew Manager for the day, looks up at the darkening sky.

Clouds gather above the port of Alexandria in the distance, a bruised vortex against the minarets of the city. Water slaps roughly on the hull. The wind picks up, the sea louder now as the turquoise Mediterranean turns to violet capped with white foam. A chill sweeps around the boat, hunting for cracks to force itself into. I shiver, pulling up my wetsuit to cover goose-pimpled flesh. The smell of decomposition wafts on the wind, dead things and offal from the rubbish barges near the shore, a stagnant rotting fish odour that makes my nose crinkle. It's been a backdrop to the summer, but I'm still not used to it, even now.

"Storm's coming." Mark looks at his watch. "It's almost the end of shift and the other boats have all headed back. Besides, you don't have a buddy. Frank's changed and sleeping down below."

Desperate thoughts run through my mind.

But I have to go down before the storm comes, before the silt of the seabed covers the city.

185

I saw something down there. The Dark Queen. I'm sure of it.

I need—

"I'll go with her."

His voice is like the edge of the abyss, a smooth oblivion that beckons to the depths. Seductive. Dangerous.

Khalid leans against the side of the boat, wetsuit half-peeled off revealing his lean torso, muscles taut and powerful, a threat made flesh. His dark eyes flash to mine.

"I'll take you down."

My mind flashes back to that night in Alexandria when the archaeological team first met for the season. He was charming at first, but he changed when we were alone. The marks on my wrists had taken weeks to fade, the bruises on my thighs ached and I had bled inside. He had laughed at my tears, confident of his position on the team. He was the main Egyptian cultural liaison, a key part of the dive expedition, and I... well, I needed to be on this trip. I'd been a junior on too many digs and my grant was over unless I could prove myself valuable this time.

Whatever the cost.

With careful management, I'd managed to avoid diving with him as a buddy, even making sure I was on a different boat most days as the excavations progressed. But today…

I need to go down there. If I find the Dark Queen…

I clench my fists and nod slowly, looking back at Mark. His decision would be final.

He nods. "Alright, but you only have thirty minutes bottom time. No longer. I mean it, Lara."

Khalid and I gear up next to each other, both of us used to the rhythm of the dive boat, both experienced divers with years of underwater archaeology between us, but my hands still shake.

He brushes my arm. I flinch away and a smile lifts the corner of his mouth.

"Which quadrant do you want to search?"

I grab the waterproof chart printed with the layout of the drowned city beneath us, holding it out in front of me, a barrier between our bodies.

"Here, between the Temple and the cemetery."

Khalid stops checking his gear and leans closer. "You seek the Dark Queen?" His voice is almost a whisper, less confident now, and there is hesitation in his eyes.

I nod. "What do you know of her?"

He looks back towards Alexandria in the distance, the edge of a country layered by myth and brutal history.

"Legend tells of a powerful Queen of this city

who ripped men apart to avenge an ancient wrong. When the streets ran thick with blood, the people called for justice. The greatest magician in Egypt trapped the Queen inside a statue and flooded the city to keep her eternal rage captive."

My thoughts race at his words. *I hear her calling to me, as she has done every night since we started diving here.*

I sense his hesitation and tilt my head to one side, eyes fixed on his, daring to challenge him. "So, you don't want to come, then?"

He shrugged. "It's just a legend." He leaned closer. "I wouldn't miss going down with you." He pulls a heavy dive knife out of its sheath with a rasp and checks the blade for nicks. He holds it casually, the knife edge towards me for a pointed second, then he thrusts it back into the sheath and attaches the weapon to his calf with its rubber strap.

Gearing up quickly, Khalid steps off the back of the boat into the choppy waves. I see dark shapes shift in the waters beneath him, shadows with teeth and tentacles waiting for prey to step into their domain.

"You going then?"

I blink and the images fade. Mark notes the time as I step into the water with a splash and swim over to Khalid, pushing away thoughts of what might be below. We both give the okay signal before sinking beneath the water.

It's dark below as the storm grows overhead and the cold penetrates my wetsuit immediately, the chill of the dead city wrapping around us. We turn on powerful torches and descend towards the ruins of what was once Egypt's greatest port. Thonis-Heracleion disappeared from history two thousand years ago, and was only rediscovered this century, a perfectly preserved ancient city buried under the silt of the Mediterranean. Archaeological dive teams cleared away much of the seabed that covered it, but as the summer season draws to a close, there is still so much left to uncover. I don't want to leave. Here is history and my place in it.

Equalizing and finding neutral buoyancy, we fin along the sea floor. I can hear the rhythmic sound of my breath and the bubbles of exhalation, the click of fish feeding. The water is full of silt, an eerie green of hanging particles that refract the light and make shadows seem much larger.

The colossal head of a god emerges from the gloom, hacked from its torso and decapitated on the sea bed, its sightless eyes staring into the deep. Fish pick at its once worshipped flesh. Around it lie scarab beetle sculptures, the devourers of the dead.

Come to me.

The voice in my head is louder now. She must be close.

The temple suddenly looms out of the dark, its massive pillars half buried in the silt. Behind it lies the cemetery where caskets of animal dead have been uncovered. Mummified ibis, their beaks like daggers, fragile bones crumbling as the air reached them. Perhaps this city was not meant to be found, after millennia under the sea.

A school of barracuda speed from the dark and whirl about us, the flash of silver bodies making me dizzy. I sink to the bottom and kneel on the sea bed, perfectly still as I look up at them. Their beady eyes gaze down, assessing potential prey, gulping at the water with strong jaws and razor teeth for ripping flesh apart. Perfect predators. There are sharks in the Mediterranean, but these fish are more terrifying. They hunt in packs and they outnumber us.

This is their domain.

My fists clench as they circle closer.

"Beautiful, aren't they?"

Khalid's voice is almost a shock in the quiet of the deep but the full face-masks make communication possible down here. Still, I don't want him intruding. I say nothing and stare up at the whirling fish.

After a moment, they pass on and I push up from the sea bed, finning towards the Temple.

A hand on my ankle tugs me back, fingers tight and bruising.

I spin and kick out at Khalid and turn to see him smile.

With the other hand, he runs his fingers up my leg. I struggle against him.

"Don't go too far." He squeezes once more and then lets me go. My heart hammers in my chest; my breath comes fast as I remember him pinning me down that night.

Is he worried that I might report him now it's the end of the season?

Could he leave me down here?

I swallow down the bile in my throat and fight to regain my composure. I can't afford to drain my air too fast. There's not enough time.

I take one more deep breath and let it out slowly before finning away, acutely aware of him behind me.

Then I know what I must do.

An ancient path winds past the temple colonnade and I swim along it, just above the sea floor. Suddenly, I give two powerful kicks, enough to disturb the thick silt, sending it in a plume in front of him, rendering him blind. I switch off my torch, turn sharp left and duck inside the temple.

The hall is half buried and the silt is thick in here,

swept in by the storm and churned in the entrance way. Unable to see, a wave of vertigo sweeps over me and for a moment, I don't know which way is up or down or how to find my way out again.

Panic rises within.

"Lara, where are you? I was only playing. I'm sorry. Come back."

Khalid's voice anchors me. I can't let him find the Dark Queen or he'll claim the find.

It has to be me — alone.

I reach out my hand and find the carvings on the wall. The horns of the Apis bull orientate me and I pull myself around and down towards the opening I saw on my last dive.

But the silt has shifted, and the entrance is too tight for me to swim through in full gear. I hesitate but if the storm continues, this might be my only chance. The temple could be buried again tomorrow.

There's only one way I can do this, but the thought makes my mouth dry and my head pound. Without a buddy, it's a huge risk.

I could be trapped in here... lose my air... drown in convulsions of agonized breath.

Help me, please.

The voice is loud in my head.

The Dark Queen is close, crushed beneath tons of silt for millennia, just waiting for me.

I pull off my BCD jacket with tank attached, keeping the regulator in my mouth. I swim into the shaft and pull the tank with one hand, a more streamlined shape now its bulk is behind me. I claw my way along the shaft, fingernails scraping on the stone. It goes on too long, too far, and the silt blinds me. Then, suddenly, the rock ends and I emerge into the inner chamber.

There's a palpable presence in here and for a moment, I don't want to turn on my torch. The dead have lain here alone for so long.

What if something else is here? What if it has been waiting?

Don't be crazy. This is your chance.

I switch my torch on, the beam turned down in case Khalid is in the outer temple. Then I see her, just a partial face emerging from the seabed, a gentle, generous smile playing around her lips, eyes unseeing as they gaze towards me. Even the tiny part of what I can see is beautiful.

I look at my dive computer. My air is low. We've been down too long, but I can't leave her now.

I scrabble at the silt around the statue, digging my fingers through the dirt that clutches her. Tiny shells slice at my flesh and blood seeps from my fingertips as I reach down through the layers of history.

Slowly, I uncover perfectly smooth skin. I touch the rise of her breasts, the silk of her dress, but her arms are still pinned. My breath comes faster now and I tear at the silt that covers her, clawing it away in great handfuls. The dust of the dead whirls in the water around me and I can hardly see now, but as I pull away the stone that crushes her arms, I see she is almost free.

The torch flickers, and her gentle smile turns cruel. Her smooth skin crumples into withered scars, diseased flesh dissolved by the ocean. The edges of a yellowed skull emerge with teeth bared in fury. I scream into my mask and push the dead thing away.

The torch light goes out.

A crushing pain around my chest as the weight of stone pins me to the bottom of the chamber, driving the air from my lungs.

Something brushes my face.

My mask is swept off.

My regulator is gone. My air is gone.

I can't breathe.

Struggling against the weight of rock above, I scan the darkness with unseeing eyes. The salt stings and presses against my throat, urging me to inhale the dead city.

I try to stop myself but the weight presses down on my chest again and I can't help it.

I gasp. Water rushes in and I gag. Convulse.

Light explodes in my mind, and I only wish it was over.

Then suddenly the weight is gone, the water is gone. I can breathe. It's as if I am born again. Oh, sweet breath. I open my eyes.

No, no. It can't be.

I'm looking at myself. I see my own face behind the dive mask. Another Lara looks back at me with a cruel smile.

A Dark Queen must always remain with the city, but each may call another to her place.

"Lara, where are you?"

Khalid's voice is worried. The glimmer of his torch pierces the gloom of the inner chamber and the Lara-who-is-not-me turns away. She drags the tank back down the tunnel towards him, leaving me in the dark, an effigy of a wronged woman.

Through the tunnel, I can just see her reach for Khalid and grasp his hand before the silt swirls around me, hiding them from sight.

"Let's go up now," she says softly. "I've been down here too long."

Her voice is my own, faint now as the two ascend together towards the silhouette of the boat far above.

The storm whips the seabed into a maelstrom of

silt, filling the inner chamber as my tomb shifts and sinks once more.

AUTHOR'S NOTE

This story is based on the Sunken Egypt exhibition at the British Museum in 2016 where objects from Thonis-Heracleion were displayed alongside details of the excavation and recovery. I had the idea for the story when I stood in front of one statue of a goddess and wondered how she might feel to escape the depths after so long.

The city of Thonis-Heracleion served as Egypt's main international trading port from around the eighth century BC until the founding of Alexandria in 331 BC. As it was located at the mouth of the Nile Delta, it was the entry point for all ships coming from the Greek world into Egypt, making it incredibly wealthy and culturally diverse.

The city gradually sank into the sea due to a combination of factors including earthquakes, tsunamis, and soil liquefaction. The soft clay and sand of the Nile Delta couldn't support the weight of the massive stone buildings and monuments, causing them to slowly submerge. By the eighth century AD, Thonis-Heracleion had completely disappeared beneath the waves.

In 2000, the site was rediscovered by the European

Institute for Underwater Archaeology (IEASM) and they have worked with Egypt's Supreme Council of Antiquities to excavate the area.

*   *   *

The Dark Queen short story was first published in *Feel The Fear* anthology (September 2017) published by WMG Publishing.

A MIDWINTER SACRIFICE

UNDER THE HEART OF the city of Bath, an ancient spring sputtered in the dark of the crypt. A few last drops of water spilled onto the stone altar, drying in russet patches over flakes of blood, layered from generations of sacrifice.

The surface of the altar was pitted and scarred, chiselled into spirals and waves in homage to the almost-forgotten goddess. While the spring flowed, she slept.

But now the waters were almost dry.

As the faint sound of Christmas carols sank down from the city above, the shadows shifted and a slight figure emerged from the rock.

The goddess needed to drink once more.

*   *   *

Evan stepped out of the hostel into the freezing morning air and pulled his faded woollen cap down over his ears. He exhaled, a cloud of breath forming in front of him.

The winter sun was warm on his skin and he looked up, closing his eyes against its brightness. The cold air stung his freshly shaven chin, the cheap Bic razor an investment in his busking routine. After all, clean shaven meant respectable.

He reached around and knocked twice on the body of the guitar case slung onto his back. The low echo thrummed through his chest, a good-luck ritual for the day. If he could play a tune that made people smile or raised a tear, then he was a musician earning proper money, not a homeless beggar. He might even earn a good feed.

Steak pie and chips. A pint of Dark and Stormy. He could almost taste it.

Evan walked away from the hostel, down the hill towards the centre of the city. The narrow modern streets opened out into wide Georgian terraces, the cream-coloured stone catching the sun as he strode past. Elaborate Christmas lights hung between lamp-posts, strings of bright red and silver curled into the shape of festive wreaths. Above them, the spire of the medieval Abbey spiked the sky. Evan pulled his battered leather jacket closer around him and stuck his hands in his pockets. He needed to keep his fingers warm to play.

A few minutes later, he emerged into the oldest part of the city, where the Christmas market sprawled between the Abbey and the ancient Roman baths. People had walked upon these stones for over two thousand years — pagan worshippers paid homage to the water goddess Sulis; Roman soldiers left curse tablets in the spa waters of Sulis Minerva;

and much later, Georgian aristocrats soaked their bloated bodies in the fashionable heart of Bath Spa.

In these modern days of secular consumerism, seasonal shoppers flocked from the surrounding counties, bringing full wallets and a festive spirit. Evan smiled as he walked across the courtyard in front of the Abbey, anticipating the generosity of the good-natured crowd. He would sleep with a full belly tonight.

An enormous Christmas tree stood in front of the Abbey, twinkling with silver lights and behind it, the imposing stone facade that housed the Christian heart of the city. Carved ladders flanked the huge stained-glass window and angels climbed toward heaven on either side, their wings tucked behind as they reached up with slender fingers. But one angel clawed its way *down* the ladder, its body slinking close to the slats, its head swivelled toward those below instead of its Lord above.

It was only a stone carving, but Evan shivered at its malevolent stare as it crawled toward him, teeth bared, long fingers like talons ready to rip him apart.

He pushed the thought away and returned to Christmas cheer, running through his repertoire of songs as he weaved his way through the warren of little wooden huts toward the busking pitch.

Artisan goods overflowed from every stall

— locally made Bath gin, West Country cheese, handmade jewellery, and Christmas wreaths woven from dried oranges and holly. The smell of mulled cider filled the air with notes of spiced apple and cinnamon. On one stall, hot roasted chestnuts crackled in sugar over flame and nearby, the scent of thick hot chocolate spiked with brandy, the sweetness making Evan's mouth water.

Smiling families dawdled by the stalls with children bundled up in puffy coats, sticky fingers clutching chocolate reindeer and Santa's special fudge.

One little girl in a red dress stopped in front of a stall with hand-carved puppets, her eyes wide as she stared into the mass of strings. Her mother pointed out a pretty pink fairy, but Evan noticed the child gazing at the dark goat-like figure of Krampus. It clutched a birch branch in one gnarled hand to beat its victims and a basket on its back to carry children away for devouring. Dark spirits lurked behind the glittering festive cliché and Evan wondered which puppet the little girl really wanted.

He walked on past a Christmas decoration stall, each little ornament in coloured glass, delicate and spun like cotton candy. One showed a little boy kneeling by a bed saying his prayers, an empty stocking next to him waiting for gifts. Something about the boy's posture made Evan catch his breath. It had been so long since he had prayed, so long since there had been a bed to kneel next to for more than a couple of nights. His own home back in Dublin had certainly been no sanctuary.

He hurried on, eyes skimming over the remaining stalls as he picked his way through the crowd. The market was suddenly too close, too loud, too bright. He needed to play, to quiet memory with music so the past would recede once more. Evan clenched his fists in his pockets. Not long now, the pitch was just up ahead.

He emerged from the crush into a square directly beneath the south flank of the Abbey, bounded on one side by the walls of the ancient Roman bath. Huts nestled around the edges selling German sausages and mulled wine, and groups of festive shoppers stood around munching while they listened to the busker finishing up his session with a Van Morrison classic. The guy was okay, but Evan knew he could warm up this pitch in no time.

A ray of winter sun broke through the clouds and touched a tiny stall nestled against the side of the Abbey. The young woman tending it had blonde hair, curled and plaited on either side of her head, an intricate design interwoven with winter holly and berries. She turned and caught Evan's eye, smiling in welcome. A friendly face was always a good start to a busking pitch, so he walked over.

A simple black cloth dominated her stall, dramatically framing a series of small round discs made from lead and stone marked with symbolic waves and curling spirals. Minimalist jewellery that seemed quite out of keeping with the extravagant colours and designs of the other stalls — but there was something about it that drew Evan in.

"Have you come for the day?" the young woman asked, her voice soft and lilting. Her eyes were almost aquamarine, a welcoming blue with a hidden promise, and she smelled fresh with a hint of something mineral.

Evan tapped his guitar. "I'm busking. Do you know how I can get a slot?"

The young woman turned and pointed toward a side door of the Abbey. "Over there. Those two guys are running things."

She touched his hand. Her skin was like water on silk, slip-sliding and smooth and cold as marble. "Be sure to come back later. Maybe we can have a glass of mulled wine after closing up."

Evan smiled. The day might turn out even better than expected. "I'll play a song for you."

He walked over to the side door, where two men leaned against stone pillars on either side of the gate, bundled up in knock-off designer jackets and black jeans. One sucked the last puff of a cigarette as Evan approached.

"I'm looking to play. You manage the pitch?"

The smoker dropped the butt of the cigarette to the flagstones, crushing it with his heel. He was silent for a few seconds and Evan sensed judgment in the man's stare. Did he see a young musician with potential, despite the rough clothes he wore?

"Do you sing as well as play?" The smoker nodded at the guitar, his accent a rough West Country.

Evan nodded. "Yes, Irish tunes as well as carols."

"No more bloody carols." The other man grunted and spat on the ground. "If you play something else, you can have the pitch next."

"I'll play folk songs then. Something different."

The smoker hawked and spat on the ground. "We take fifty percent. Bring it here after your slot."

That was robbery and they all knew it. But the man's eyes were as hard as the frost on newly dug graves.

Evan nodded.

The smoker pointed out into the square. "Take over from that loser. Maybe the luck of the Irish will bring you some more cash."

As Evan walked out into the middle of the square, the clouds parted and the late winter sun blessed the gathered masses with its warmth. The anticipation of performance warmed him inside, and his fingers itched for the vibration of that first note. Even the potential of losing half his earnings couldn't dampen his anticipation of the smiling crowd — and the chink of coins in his guitar case.

He stood for a second in the middle of the square, silently calling the masses to him in a ritual he performed before any busking session. Turn and listen, turn and listen.

Evan swung his guitar around and touched the strings, the pads of his fingers tingling from the cold but also with his need to play.

He plucked the first chords, caressing the strings as he sang of a home beyond the waves, a time of magic, and love that conquered all. He smiled as he sang, catching the eyes of the shoppers, weaving them into the music. This was when he felt most alive, and it didn't matter that he had little in the world. When the melody soared, he was happy.

A little girl ran forward with a few coins and then more people dropped money in his guitar case, nodding at him and clapping as he finished each tune.

Evan sang on and soon his case overflowed with donations and Christmas cheer and a few pieces of fudge for good measure.

But as the clock struck four and the early winter darkness clawed its way over the city, a freezing wind swept into the square.

The clouds broke apart.

Icy sleet poured down, and the wind swept a blizzard into the Christmas huts.

People scurried for shelter, grabbing the hands of their children and running for the bigger shops on the high street. The hut owners slammed their shutters closed, trying to protect their stock from the sudden storm. The sound of hail on stone echoed through the suddenly empty square.

Evan snapped his guitar case shut and picked it up in one hand while he hugged his guitar to his chest with the other.

He ran for shelter, ducking down an alleyway at the side of the Abbey. He cowered in a doorway, turning inwards to protect his precious instrument from the icy rain. A drop of freezing water ran down the back of his neck and he shivered as he waited for the storm to pass.

The sound of heavy footsteps came from the alleyway behind.

Evan whipped his head around to see the two men approaching, oblivious to the storm raging about them, their hard eyes fixed on his guitar case.

"You running with our money?" the smoker growled.

Evan shook his head. "I was just sheltering from the storm. I can go back out when it stops. It's a good pitch. I'll get more."

The smoker stepped forward, crushing Evan into the corner of the doorway. His breath stank of stale smoke and cheap brandy. "The day's over, so we'll take it now. All of it."

"Fifty percent, you said."

The man gave a grim smile, and Evan glimpsed faraway places in his grey eyes. Forests of tall trees and pale graves beneath mounds of dark earth where fresh corpses lay inches beneath the surface.

The smoker grabbed Evan's coat and jerked him forward, smashing the bridge of Evan's nose with a practiced head butt.

As pain exploded through his skull and blood gushed in a warm stream, Evan fell to his knees, gasping for breath as drops of red speckled the flagstones beneath him.

The other man leaned in and grabbed for the guitar case.

Evan wrestled to keep hold of it. He dug his fingers in, tugging it back towards his torso. The cash was the only thing keeping him from the streets tonight.

The smoker kicked him hard.

The blow thudded against Evan's ribs and he fell back against his guitar, the sound of splintering wood an echo of his despair.

He let the case go, but the men didn't stop.

The two of them laid into him, their swift blows aimed with expertise and deliberation. Evan curled up on the freezing ground, his arms wrapped around his head, waiting for it to end. The sound of their panting breath was almost drowned out by the pounding of rain on stone, the thuds resounding through his bruised body, pain cresting as he wished for the darkness to come.

As the edge of oblivion beckoned, the men stopped.

Evan reached for his guitar. If he could just…

The smoker said something guttural and the other man laughed. He grabbed the guitar and stomped on it, his heavy boots breaking the wood, splintering it to pieces on the stones beneath.

The men walked away, and Evan curled around the remains of his livelihood. He wanted to sink into the freezing cold earth and let the pain dissolve with him. There was nothing left. He had lost the only thing that earned him a meal and a bed. The only thing that brought him joy and could banish the memories he ran from.

He cursed the two men, the words of his Celtic ancestors coming unbidden to his lips. Incantations he had heard in dark places far away from the church, whispered maledictions that spoke of sacrifice to those of ancient times.

As he lay in the dark, Evan's blood pooled in the furrows between the flagstones, trickling down to the ancient spring beneath.

The storm passed, but Evan lay unmoving, the cold numbing his bruised limbs as he focused on each breath that filled his lungs. On every exhalation, he cursed the men who had taken everything from him.

Soft footsteps approached from the end of the alley.

"Oh no. You poor thing." The young woman from the market stall ran over and knelt next to him.

She brushed his wet, matted hair from his face and touched his wounds with cool fingers, staining her fingernails with his blood.

Evan looked up at her concerned expression. How could he have thought her eyes were a welcoming aquamarine? They were cold and clear as a crystal spring now, a reflection of the winter storm.

"They took everything. Even my guitar is ruined." He stifled a sob.

"Shh," the young woman whispered. "I have something that can help you." Her voice was sharper now, like the edge of rough-cut flint. "The goddess of the spring hears those who call on her."

Evan's breath caught in his throat, as if a sliver of ice pierced his heart and disrupted its rhythm.

He had spoken his own curses only minutes before, and this was a place of power, a sacred spring for thousands of years and a convergence point for Druidic ley lines that ran all the way to Stonehenge.

"What should I do?"

She smiled. "Come with me."

Evan stood slowly, using the wall of the abbey to push himself up. He leaned on the young woman and they hobbled together back down the alleyway to her stall. The market square was deserted now, the colourful Christmas lights casting an eerie glow onto the stone.

The young woman pointed at the carved discs of stone and lead marked with pagan runes, some curled and spiny, others with slash marks and deep cuts. "These are curse tablets."

One in particular drew Evan's gaze. A piece of bullet-grey lead marked with a deep slash bisected with smaller slices, as if claws had raked across its surface in a haze of bloodlust.

"Take it," she whispered.

Evan picked it up and let the cool weight lie in his palm. It seemed to pulse with a dark vein of power that connected him to the earth below and the sky above with some kind of elemental force. In a moment of clarity, he glimpsed how insignificant he was against the timelessness of this ancient place, and a sense of vertigo almost sent him to his knees.

But he couldn't let it go.

Evan imagined casting it into the spring and as it settled on the bottom in the dark, tendrils of rust would spiral from it as the curse worked its magic.

He looked at the young woman. "I... I can't pay for it."

She put a cool finger against his lips, her touch feather-light. "The curse tablet chooses its own. This one is yours. Offer it to the goddess and she will take her sacrifice. The spring is this way."

She ducked back behind her stall and Evan followed, the pain in his body ebbing away as his curiosity grew.

There was a stone staircase in the Abbey wall. He could have sworn it hadn't been there earlier, and yet it looked archaic. The steps had a slope in the middle, worn from so many desperate feet over millennia, trekking down to the spring in supplication. How many came for vengeance? How many saw their curses fulfilled?

Evan took a step down and clutched at the stone wall to steady his wobbly legs. As he descended, he looked back up at the woman. Her eyes were like an ice cave now, reminiscent of the blue light in the centre of an ancient glacier. How could he have thought her so young?

"Aren't you coming with me?"

"You'll find the way," she answered, her voice like the ripple of a hidden creature under a pool of dark water.

Evan clutched his curse token and turned back to the stairway, winding his way down to a fissure in the rock, a semblance of a doorway that led inexorably down. The sound of dripping water came from within and he walked carefully toward where he thought the spring must be, using the freezing stone for guidance in the gloom.

It felt timeless down here, as if the air had frozen in an older age when people lived closer to the earth and its spirits. Evan felt an urge to turn back, to ascend to the realm of Christmas lights and sugar candy and tinsel and holiday cheer.

But the curse tablet burned in his hand with cool fire and he could smell the mineral scent of the pool, somehow reminiscent of the woman above.

He must be close now.

There was a light up ahead, a deep green haze as if he swam beneath thick fronds of seaweed in the shadows of the deep.

Evan edged around a last bend in the tight corridor and emerged into a stone chamber roughly hewn from the rock. There were marks on the walls, curling and spiky and slashed like the curse tablets and in the centre, a low altar where once the sacred waters had overflowed with abundance.

But now the spring was dry.

Evan's heart pounded as he approached the altar. There were patches of something dark on the rock — could it be blood?

A statue of the goddess of the spring stood behind the altar. The hazy green light flickered across her delicate features, illuminating her curled and plaited hair, an intricate design interwoven with winter holly and berries.

She smiled down at him and as the light faded to black, it seemed as if her marble lips parted in anticipation.

Evan turned to run.

He slipped on the wet stone and fell to his knees, pain slamming through his already broken body.

He crawled on, desperate to escape, but he could no longer find the fissure he entered through. He scraped against the stone, his fingers bleeding as he tried to claw the rock apart.

"Help! Let me out!" he shouted up to the market above, but the thick stone smothered his cries until he fell sobbing to the cold stone beneath.

In the dark, Evan heard the whisper of water slipping toward him over the cracked floor of the ancient spring. A cool finger softly touched his lips and soothed his wounds with icy balm before slipping into his throat, pouring ice into his lungs, silencing his final scream.

The goddess drank and, under the heart of the city, the ancient spring bubbled into life once more.

AUTHOR'S NOTE

I first wrote this story inspired by the Bath Christmas markets back in 2015, but I didn't publish it because I wanted Evan to triumph and emerge from his difficult situation into a better life.

But every time I revisited the story, his path always ended in sacrifice.

A single life given for the benefit of all.

It's not fair — and it's not how I wanted the story to go — but that's just how it is sometimes.

As I re-edited the story again in mid-December 2021, we were living in the COVID-19 pandemic. Every single person sacrificed something for the greater good — and it was still not over.

The darkness of *A Midwinter Sacrifice* felt appropriate when I finally published it, and I released this story into the world with a glimmer of hope. Perhaps the goddess had taken enough, and our collective spring would bubble into life once more.

* * *

At the time of writing, I live in Bath, England, and the setting of the Christmas market next to the Abbey and the Roman baths is accurate.

Every year the council build a warren of little huts and people come from around the area to shop, and drink mulled cider and eat juicy burgers. There are plenty of beautiful handmade gifts and moments of Christmas cheer — but the market also has dark corners.

There are indeed curse tablets in the museum at the Roman Baths, pulled from the hot springs and inscribed with words of power. The Celtic goddess Sulis was once worshipped here, before the Romans assimilated her into Sulis Minerva, and then the Christians built a simple church, and then an Abbey on the sacred site.

I've explored the city's pagan and occult side further through my Mapwalker dark fantasy trilogy, starting with *Map of Shadows*.

You can listen to me talk about *Druids, Freemasons, and Frankenstein: The Darker Side of Bath, England*, in an episode of my *Books and Travel Podcast*:

www.booksandtravel.page/bath-england

DE-EXTINCTION OF THE NEPHILIM

They have gone to the daughters of men upon the earth, and have slept with the women, and have defiled themselves, and revealed to them all kinds of sins. And the women have borne giants, and the whole earth has thereby been filled with blood and unrighteousness.

—The Book of Enoch, Apocrypha, 4:6

We have the DNA, the technology and the leading experts in the field. Next, we will have the woolly mammoth. Alive again.

—Colossal Laboratories & Biosciences, colossal.com/mammoth

CHAPTER 1

AS THE FIRST LIGHT of dawn crept over the horizon, Dr Emilia Kaya emerged from her tent at the edge of the Göbekli Tepe archaeological site in the grasslands of south-eastern Turkey. The air was still cool, but the promise of another scorching day lay ahead. She could only hope that this day would be different because her funding was near to running out, and so was this dig season.

She inhaled deeply, savouring the scent of dry earth and wild herbs as she listened to the distant chirping of birds and the soft rustle of wind through the sparse vegetation. A rare moment of stillness before the excavation day began.

Emilia stretched her arms up and cricked her neck, suppressing a groan at the familiar ache of muscles stretched taut from long hours of digging and crouching over ancient remains.

As Director of Border Excavations, she really should delegate the physical labour to the keen students and the more junior archaeologists, but even after all her years in the field, she still loved to feel dirt beneath her fingernails. Even on such a developed site as Göbekli Tepe, there were still mysteries to be uncovered.

The night sky faded to a lighter blue, and Emilia turned to look out over the main excavation site. Ancient ruins rose from the earth with massive T-shaped pillars that predated the pyramids of Egypt and the standing stones of Stonehenge. The carvings on the limestone — depictions of animals, symbols, and anthropomorphic figures — caught the morning light, casting long, shifting shadows that danced across the ground in a semblance of life.

Despite the years of excavation and study, much about Göbekli Tepe remained a mystery. Who were the people who built it, and what was its purpose? Was it a temple, a burial ground, or something else entirely?

She looked at her watch. Her second in command, Dr Mehmet Ali, would be on his way from the nearby town of Şanlıurfa, hopefully with a bag of delicious savoury poğaça pastries.

Mehmet preferred the more comfortable off-site lodgings, but Emilia had worked late last night on the final plans for the chamber entrance and hadn't wanted to leave the site. Besides, there was something special about spending the night here, watching the stars that people had gazed up at eleven thousand years ago when this site had been built. Perhaps this morning they would discover an answer to at least one of the mysteries that lay beneath her feet.

Emilia and Mehmet had worked together on many digs, and his expertise in geophysical survey-ing had helped identify an anomaly on ground-penetrating radar scans. While the main site of Göbekli Tepe was a major tourist attraction these days, with its primary buildings fully excavated, Emilia led a small team expanding the borders of the original dig.

She had always been fascinated by puzzles — she could never leave a crossword unfinished — and the markings on one particular pillar had intrigued her enough to request funding for this summer project. But it was only enough for one season. In order to continue, they had to find something that would justify future support.

After months of careful excavation, their patience had been rewarded, and today she and Mehmet would enter the chamber they'd discovered yesterday.

It had lain undisturbed for centuries, perhaps even millennia, and they wanted to go in early, alone, before the site grew busy. Yesterday, they had finally been ready to enter the portal of the complex they'd uncovered but, after traversing a short pas-sageway, they'd found a huge stone door blocking further progress. After cutting an exploratory hole, they had done an initial safety assessment, testing the atmosphere inside with a miniature drone and getting some first film of what lay within. There must be vents to the surface, as the air was breathable with no measurable pathogens, but the images of the interior were too blurry to make out anything in particular. Emilia itched to get inside.

The sound of footsteps crunching on gravel made her turn.

Mehmet climbed the path toward her, a cloth bag in one hand and a large thermos in the other. He waved.

"*Günaydın*, Emilia. I come bearing gifts."

"You're a lifesaver. I'm famished." The warm, buttery aroma of the cheesy poğaça pastry reached her as he approached, and Emilia's stomach rumbled in anticipation. "Let's eat them at the entrance."

Together they walked to the edge of the main site, and through the security barriers set up to keep curious tourists away from the active dig.

They sat down at the entrance to the newly excavated passageway, settling themselves on the worn stone steps. Mehmet unscrewed the top of the thermos and poured out two small cups of thick Turkish coffee, pungent with cardamom.

Emilia cradled hers in both hands, letting the

heat seep into her fingers as she gazed down at the archway before them.

The massive stone portal was carved with intricate symbols — whorls and eddies that suggested surging flood waters, as well as what looked like heavy linked chains. There were columns of text in a language reminiscent of cuneiform, yet no one had been able to decipher it, despite the many experts she'd consulted. A warning perhaps, or the tale of this ancient site. The carvings on the arch hinted at dark myths, at angry gods and towering giants. What if some element of truth lay behind those legends? The only way to find out was to get inside.

They sipped their coffee in companionable silence as the sun climbed higher. After a few minutes, a shaft of light hit the top of the archway, illuminating the carvings in sharp relief.

It was time.

They gathered their gear, slinging on backpacks filled with water, flashlights, and excavation tools. Emilia nodded to Mehmet and together they walked down the steps and pulled back the heavy tarpaulin covering the entrance, folding it carefully to one side.

Emilia clicked on her flashlight and ducked her head to step through the archway, Mehmet a few steps behind.

The passageway sloped downward at a gentle angle, the walls just far enough apart that they could walk without brushing the sides. The floor beneath their feet was cut directly into bedrock, worn into channels by the passage of dripping water.

Emilia ran her fingertips along the wall, tracing the chisel marks left by ancient masons. She felt as though she walked back in time with every step, shedding the modern world like a second skin, and her sense of anticipation began to rise. She had kept it in check for the long months of careful excavation, but now, with just days left in the season, she was determined to find something. These tunnels alone were not enough to get renewed funding.

She needed more.

Beside her, Mehmet's breath quickened. "I'm trying not to get excited," he said, his voice unnaturally loud in the narrow tunnel. "But I can't help feeling that we will be the first in decades to discover something new here. Your grandfather would have been proud."

Emilia nodded. "I wish he could have been here to see it."

Her grandfather had been an uneducated man who worked his whole life as a labourer on Turkish archaeological digs. He had brought home stories of wonders he had helped uncover at Ephesus and

Hattusa, and little Emilia had imagined discovering new places that would make his eyes shine once more. Her family had worked incredibly hard to fund her education and, although her grandfather had died before she made her own discoveries, she was still determined to make him proud.

The air grew colder as they descended, and Emilia felt goosebumps prickle along her arms despite the layers she wore. The passage narrowed, and the ceiling lowered until they were forced to stoop. Finally, it opened up into an antechamber.

Emilia played her flashlight over the walls, the beam illuminating more of the unusual script, with the same swirling flood waters and heavy chains carved in spiralling patterns that seemed to lead toward a stone door.

It was thick and solid, with no visible handle or hinges. They couldn't blast down here, so they had decided to cut through the stone. Mehmet had already supervised the initial excavation and safety tests, and now he bent to the hole in the corner of the door.

"It won't take much to enlarge it enough so we can wriggle through."

They unslung their packs and pulled out chisels and hammers. Emilia selected a chisel and placed the tip against the stone near the edge of the hole, angling it carefully. The first strike of the hammer sent a jolt up her arm and a spray of dust into the air.

They worked steadily, taking turns at chipping away the stone, and soon, the small antechamber filled with the sound of metal on rock and their laboured breathing. They peeled off layers as they worked up a sweat, and Emilia revelled in the simple act of excavation, her sense of expectation growing with every minute.

Finally, Mehmet took a step back to survey the gap. "I think that's as much as we dare remove. Any more and we risk destabilising the entire structure." He raised an eyebrow and grinned. "Besides, even with the pastries, I think we'll both fit through."

Emilia shone her flashlight into the hole, angling it to see into the chamber beyond. The beam played over a stone floor, thick with dust and debris. There were visible pillars and something beyond, just out of reach of the light.

She took a deep breath. "Let's do it."

She got down on hands and knees and eased herself into the gap, trying not to think about the tons of rock over her head and how they might have weakened the heavy door. The rough stone scraped against her palms as she rotated to allow for the slight curve of her hips.

Her hands touched the ground on the other side, the first human contact for possibly millennia.

Suddenly desperate to get through, Emilia pushed with her feet, and emerged into the chamber.

She crawled forward a few meters, and Mehmet soon emerged behind her, coughing a little from the dust. He tugged the packs through after him and pulled out his phone, filming as Emilia shone her flashlight around.

A towering stone pillar rose out of the gloom, and beyond it another, and another, disappearing into darkness in two parallel rows. More of the strange script flowed across every surface, wrapping around the pillars and spiralling up to a ceiling lost in shadow.

Emilia played her torch over the nearest pillar, carved with a larger, more detailed version of the giant in chains depicted above the surface. It had fierce features and huge outstretched wings, and before it cowered a group of tiny figures on their knees. Were they worshipping or begging for mercy? It was hard to tell.

Her light flickered across the sharp edges of something between the pillars up ahead. "This way."

Emilia's heart pounded as they walked beyond the pillars, the thrill of discovery rising within her as the shape emerged from the gloom.

It was a sarcophagus, much larger than anything she had seen at other dig sites. Maybe three or four times the size of the largest sarcophagi she'd seen in Egypt.

The stone was a dark, mottled grey, carved with the same intricate patterns as the pillars. And in the centre, picked out in bold relief, was the image of the winged giant in chains.

Emilia reached out a trembling hand to touch the stone, half expecting it to be warm, or to pulse with some ancient, unknowable energy. But it was just rock, cool and unyielding beneath her fingertips. Whatever had once lain within was probably dust, but she felt an overwhelming urge to see inside.

"We need to wait," Mehmet said, sensing her desire. "I'll get the testing equipment down here. We'll do it properly, carefully."

"We don't have time." Emilia turned to meet his gaze. "There are only days left in the season, and the chamber, the carvings — they're not enough. You know I'm right."

She slowly circled the sarcophagus. "There must be a crack or a way inside without damaging it too much. Let's just have a look."

Mehmet reached out his hand and touched her arm. "We need to be careful. We don't know what we're dealing with here."

She shook him off. "We know enough. This vault is older than anything we've ever seen, and clearly it's a sacred place. We know that whatever is in this sarcophagus was important enough to be buried here, in the heart of the complex." She pointed at the pillar with the giant's image. "And that has to mean something."

She looked up at Mehmet, understanding his warring impulses of caution and curiosity. "Please. Just a little look and then we'll proceed properly if we find anything."

For a long moment, he hesitated, clearly torn. Then, slowly, he nodded. "Okay. But I won't film such bad archaeological practice, and you promise to only look. Agreed?"

"Agreed."

They worked quickly, circling the sarcophagus in different directions, probing at the seam of the lid.

"Here," Mehmet called out a minute later.

Emilia dashed round to the other side.

There was a crack in the stone. It wouldn't take much to widen it. She grabbed her chisel and fitted it to the seam, her heart racing with a mix of excitement and trepidation.

She tapped on the end of the chisel with the flat edge of her stone hammer, the sound ringing out harsh and loud in the stillness of the chamber. Flakes of rock flew, dust billowing in the torchlight.

She tapped a little harder.

With a crack like a gunshot, the chisel broke through.

Now Emilia had the sense of how deep to go, it didn't take much to make a slightly bigger gap. After a few more taps, she put down her chisel and shone her torch within.

She gasped as she struggled to process what lay inside.

The skeleton was enormous, easily ten feet long, from the top of its skull to the tips of its outstretched toes. The limbs were elongated, the bones thick and robust, and the skull was shaped like nothing she had ever seen, its cranial sutures arranged in an unfamiliar pattern. And there, arching from enormous shoulder blades, the remnants of what could only be wings.

The giant from the carvings was a real creature, perhaps a mutant, or a different species altogether. No known hominid species, ancient or modern, had this skeletal structure. The discovery could challenge the very foundations of human evolution.

"What is it?" Mehmet asked.

Emilia stepped back to let him see.

Mehmet bent to the gap and then reeled away, his eyes wide as he let out a shaky breath. "*Tanrım, bu nedir?* What is this?"

Emilia shook her head. "I don't know, but this will carve our names into the history books alongside the greatest archaeologists." She smiled, her eyes shining with triumph at the thought of what would come. "This is just the beginning. We did it, Mehmet. We did it!"

She bent back down to look again in the gap, unable to tear her gaze away from the impossible sight. Half-formed thoughts and a thousand questions whirled through her mind as she imagined establishing a new centre for archaeology here in the Middle East.

She tried to reach inside, but only managed to touch the edge of one bone with a fingertip. The gap needed to be bigger if she was to retrieve a whole specimen.

As she pulled her fingers back, a sudden low rumble shook the chamber. Dust rained down from the ceiling high above.

"Earthquake." Mehmet picked up their packs. "We need to get out of here. You know the drill."

Emilia hesitated. The bones were tantalisingly close. "It's probably another team excavating early with a small blast. Let's just wait a minute. I need a closer look."

While the region's geological past included volcanic activity, there were no recent warnings of seismic issues in the area. They had protocols in place for such an occasion, but Emilia had never used them in all her years on site.

She placed her chisel against the stone and tapped gently until the gap widened, now big enough to reach inside.

Another rumble rocked the chamber, stronger this time. Larger chunks of rock rained down.

"We have to go!" Mehmet barked, turning toward the entrance. "Move!"

As he hurried away, Emilia remained by the sarcophagus. There was so much at stake. She needed proof.

"Emilia!"

Mehmet's distant shout snapped her out of momentary paralysis. She reached inside the gap and snatched a long finger bone from the skeleton's outstretched hand, shoving it into her pocket.

The rumble became a roar.

The ground heaved and bucked beneath her feet. Chunks of stone thudded down, one landing heavily on the top of the sarcophagus, cracking the lid.

Emilia ran, stumbling as she reached the broken doorway.

Mehmet was already on the other side. "Hurry!" he called back through.

As Emilia jammed herself into the door gap, a massive crack came from behind her, then the sound of falling rock, of tonnes of stone crashing to the floor of the chamber.

Mehmet grabbed her arms and pulled Emilia through. They ran, half climbing, half crawling, as the stone shuddered and shifted around them. Emilia's lungs burned, her eyes streamed from the dust — and from the bitter knowledge that what had lain in the chamber must now be crushed beneath tons of rock.

She staggered on, coughing in the choking haze. Mehmet's hand closed around her arm as he dragged her on and up.

They finally stumbled into the blinding sunlight, gulping great lungfuls of hot, dry air.

Minutes later, the earthquake subsided; the ground steadied beneath their feet. Emilia stood next to the arched entrance to the passageway, now almost completely covered by meters of dislodged earth and rocks.

She fell to her knees, head in her hands, tears running down her cheeks.

Their months of work, the careful excavation, all lay in ruins. She would need new funding to re-excavate, and even with Mehmet's initial film of the high-ceilinged chamber, she doubted anyone would want to try again.

There was no evidence of the giant skeletal remains. She only had the bone in her pocket, and that was not enough. It looked human after all — but it wasn't. Emilia was sure of it.

She pulled the bone from her pocket and gazed down at its pitted surface. It could hold the key to resurrecting her career.

If she could get its DNA sequenced and prove it wasn't human, that might be evidence enough to get new funding, to fully excavate the site properly, and uncover what was left of the skeleton. Her old genetics professor might be able to help, and that gave Emilia a glimmer of hope and the strength to carry on.

She took a deep breath. She would make her grandfather proud. It would just take a little more time.

CHAPTER 2

THE STERILE AIR IN the lab hummed with the gentle whir of centrifuges and the soft rhythmic beep of sequencers. Dr Alexander Novak hunched over his workbench, analysing the strings of genetic code on his screen as he flipped between windows, comparing the freshly extracted thylacine DNA — from a Tasmanian tiger — to reference genomes.

Across the pristine white bench, his lab technician Yumi carefully pipetted clear liquid into a rack of tiny tubes. Her movements were precise yet tentative, her inexperience clear in the slight tremble of her hand.

"Make sure you change tips between each sample," Alex instructed. "Cross-contamination is the enemy of good science."

"Yes, Dr Novak," Yumi replied softly, without looking up from her focused intensity.

Alex allowed himself a small smile. Yumi's dedication reminded him of his own passion at that age, before years of repetitious work and pointless lab politics had ground it down. He'd taken this job at Extinct Origin BioLabs in Boston to escape the confines of academia, but most of the time, it was beneath his level of expertise and boring as hell.

He turned back to the screen, his eyes tracing the colourful lines of the thylacine DNA sequence.

The genetic material was remarkably well-preserved, considering its age. This sample had been recovered from a young thylacine pup, a Tasmanian tiger, pickled in ethanol by a forward-thinking museum curator over a century ago, when the species was already teetering on the brink of extinction.

Alex marvelled at the foresight of those early twentieth-century scientists. Their meticulous preservation of specimens, driven more by curiosity than any inkling of the biotechnological advances to come, had made his work possible. Because of them, the thylacine had a chance to live again. But even with the best samples, piecing together a full genome was a painstaking process.

The DNA was fragmented, broken into countless tiny pieces by the ravages of time and imperfect preservation methods. It was up to Alex and his team to meticulously reassemble the fragments, using innovative sequencing technology and complex computational algorithms. The latter grew more advanced every month with the rapid development of artificial intelligence and synthetic biology, and Alex wondered how much longer humans would be needed in the loop.

But for now at least, he had a job, and once they had a complete digital blueprint of the thylacine genome, the real work would begin.

They would compare it to the genomes of close living relatives, like the Tasmanian devil and the banded anteater, to fill in any gaps and correct for errors. Then would come the careful work of gene editing, tweaking the code to optimise it for the process of de-extinction.

Alex specialised in identifying key genes responsible for unique adaptations. For the thylacine that included its powerful jaws, striped coat, and marsupial pouch. Those genes needed to be intact and functional in the resurrected genome.

Once the genetic blueprint was perfected, they would inject it into a host egg cell, likely from a Tasmanian devil or another close marsupial relative. The egg would be implanted into a surrogate mother, where it would hopefully develop into a healthy thylacine joey — and the species would live again.

It was a long and complex process, fraught with challenges and ethical questions. The company tried to avoid any religious issues by using the word 'de-extinction' instead of 'resurrection,' but what were they really doing if not playing god?

This kind of frontier science reached into the

past, plucked species from the oblivion of extinction, and hauled them into the present where they no longer belonged. Even if their extinction was unfortunate, the timeline of history and evolution had continued without them, and who could know the impact of such a reversal?

Alex shook his head, thinking of the corporate bigwigs who funded the research. They loved to throw around buzzwords like 're-wilding' and 'ecosystem restoration,' painting a rose-tinted picture of a future where long-lost species roamed the earth once more.

But it was all about the bottom line in the end. Resurrected mammoths and thylacines were big-ticket attractions, living novelties that would draw in crowds and investment dollars.

These people seemed to have no comprehension of the potential consequences of their actions. Hadn't they seen *Jurassic Park*? That movie was practically a parable, a cautionary tale about the dangers of meddling with nature's course. "Life will find a way" indeed, as Michael Crichton wrote — although, of course, the book was much better than the movie.

Those at the top were too blinded by the promise of profit to heed its warning, and if Alex were honest, the money was too good to make a fuss about it. Lord knows he needed the money.

He glanced over at Yumi as he meticulously prepared samples for sequencing. She was of a different generation and believed wholeheartedly in the company's mission. The future of conservation was not just protecting the species we still had, but bringing back the ones we'd lost. Extinction need not be forever, and that was a hopeful message the young needed to hear. But like the promised reversal of climate change, Alex considered it another damaging fantasy peddled by eco-technological ideologues.

His phone pinged with an incoming message. His private email, not his work address.

Alex pulled out his phone and clicked through. A familiar name jumped out at him: Dr Emilia Kaya.

He remembered the brilliant young archaeologist who had taken his advanced genetic analysis course years ago as a minor subject to help with her fieldwork.

He opened the message.

Dear Dr Novak, I'm sorry it's been so long. I tracked you down online and it looks like you're doing well at Extinct Origins. I read that you also do private DNA consultancy. I have a favour to ask, and a bottle of Macallan Double Cask waiting on your reply. I seem to remember that's one of your favourites.

I'm working in Turkey at Göbekli Tepe, and as part of the excavation, I found a bone fragment that I don't recognise. I was hoping you might be able to extract and sequence any surviving DNA, and perhaps even identify its origin.

Please let me know if this is something you'd be willing to take on. It would be of immense help.

All the best, and many thanks,

Emilia

P.S. Please keep this confidential as I am pre-publication.

Alex leaned back in his chair, intrigued by her message.

He clicked over to LinkedIn and checked her profile. Emilia was now a well-connected senior Director of Excavations. She must know plenty of people in Turkey or further in Europe who could do such sequencing, and yet, she had reached out to him. Interesting, indeed.

He pulled up Google and searched for Göbekli Tepe, paging through pictures of the site. Looking at its towering pillars, carved with strange symbols arrayed in cryptic patterns, he imagined dark rituals performed there millennia ago. Perhaps the specimen was from something sacrificed at the site or from one of the ancient peoples who lived there.

But Emilia wouldn't need his help for something so elementary. It must be something far more curious.

He typed a reply.

Emilia, Good to hear from you. I'm intrigued. Send the sample over. Details for the courier attached. Let's see what secrets this bone of yours holds.

Regards, Alex

CHAPTER 3

TWENTY-FOUR HOURS AFTER sending his reply, Alex was back in the lab earlier than usual. The sun had barely crested the horizon, casting a pale golden light through the high windows. It was quiet, the usual hum of the busy lab not yet at full volume. The perfect time for uninterrupted work.

Just as he settled down at his bench, security at the front desk rang up.

"There's a courier package for you down here."

Alex felt a buzz of expectation as he hurried down to the entrance.

One of the night guards was inspecting an insulated box marked with bold red letters: FRAGILE. BIOHAZARD.

Alex reached out. "I'll take that, thanks."

He rushed back upstairs and placed the box on his workbench, then carefully sliced through the packing tape with a scalpel. Inside, nestled among layers of foam insulation, was a smaller box, also bearing biohazard stickers.

He put on a pair of nitrile gloves and gently lifted it out, placing it on the sterile surface of the bench. He removed the lid.

There, cushioned in yet more insulation, lay the bone.

At first glance, it appeared to be a human finger bone — a proximal phalange, likely from the middle finger, judging by its length — and the surface was pitted and weathered with age.

But as Alex gently lifted it from its packaging, he realised there was something very wrong with that assessment.

The bone was enormous.

It dwarfed any human phalange he'd ever seen, easily three times the size of a typical adult male's and much more dense. It would have supported considerably more muscle than a normal man's finger, making the hand span enormous.

"What in the world...?" Alex turned the bone over in his gloved hands. Could it be from a human with gigantism?

In some extreme cases, a pituitary tumour could lead to unchecked growth hormone production. But no, the proportions were all wrong. The bone was too thick, too robust. This wasn't just a scaled-up human bone. It was something else entirely.

A new species, perhaps? Some previously unknown hominin, a giant cousin to *Homo sapiens*? Or something stranger?

Emilia had clearly sent the bone to him knowing

it was not human, and a bottle of Macallan, however premium, was definitely not enough to solve this mystery. He would need to be a co-author on whatever academic paper she must be writing. Alex felt a flicker of excitement. This could be a late breakthrough in his career, a way to earn acclaim he had so narrowly missed out on before.

He should take the bone home and analyse it on his personal equipment, but Alex was eager to extract a sample and dive into its genetic secrets as soon as possible. The equipment here was state-of-the-art, leagues beyond what he had in his home lab. He could have results in hours, rather than days. No one would even know.

The sound of the lab door opening broke into his racing thoughts.

Alex looked up to see Yumi hanging her coat on the rack.

"Good morning, Dr Novak," she said brightly. "You're in early."

"Morning, I had a few things to work on, that's all."

Yumi approached his bench, her eyes lighting up as she saw the bone. "Is that a new sample? Are we starting a new project?"

"It's something I'm looking into for one of the other teams. Nothing for you to worry about. Can

THE BURIED AND THE DROWNED

you continue with the thylacine samples without me today?"

Yumi beamed, almost glowing with the responsibility. "Yes, of course, Dr Novak. I'll do it exactly the way you showed me. I won't let you down."

As she bustled around the lab preparing for the day's work, Alex turned his attention to the finger bone.

He began the painstaking process of extraction, carefully drilling into the weathered surface to get a sample of the genetic material within. He worked with practiced efficiency, his hands steady. The tiny drill whirred softly as he collected the bone powder and transferred it to a sterile tube.

Next, he added a buffered solution to dissolve the calcium and release the DNA. After an hour incubating with gentle agitation and centrifugation, Alex decanted the supernatant containing the genetic material into a fresh tube.

Using a microspectrophotometer, he checked the concentration and purity of the DNA. He almost expected it to return a null result. Non-degraded DNA was a lot to ask of a bone sample from a site over eleven thousand years old.

After a moment, the machine beeped, and Alex raised an eyebrow at the result.

Not only was there a surprisingly high quantity of

250

DNA, but it was largely intact, with minimal degradation. This bone, ancient as it was, harboured astonishingly well-preserved genetic material.

Now he just had to figure out what it belonged to.

He prepared a sample and added it to the sequencer. The machine whirred to life, beginning the process of unravelling the bone's genetic mystery.

Alex stood up and walked to the door, checking that Yumi still worked diligently in her corner on the other side of the lab.

She looked up and smiled. He raised a hand and ducked out the door, heading for the coffee shop down the road. He couldn't work on anything else right now. He was too distracted.

* * *

A few hours later, Alex returned to the lab, his mind still buzzing with the possibilities of what the mysterious bone could be, and how it might lead his career to new heights.

As he entered the lab, he noticed a note left by Yumi on his workbench. Her precise handwriting detailed the progress she'd made with the thylacine samples — all the steps completed exactly as per his instructions.

He looked over at the sequencer. The display showed that the run was complete.

Alex sat down and navigated to the results file, a seemingly endless string of A's, T's, C's, and G's, formatted into specific areas for further analysis.

He frowned as he checked the data.

There was no exact match. This wasn't just an unknown individual, but an unknown species. He leaned closer, studying the alignment with human DNA. There were overlaps, but also significant divergences.

As he delved deeper into the genetic code, a particular sequence caught his eye, one he'd seen before in comparative studies. It was a signature associated with wing development in mammals, particularly in bats. But the implications here were staggering.

If this creature had wings, they would have been enormous, based on the size of the bone. Alex considered the possibility of giant winged hominids. It seemed impossible, like something out of a horror novel.

He shook his head, trying to focus.

There had to be a rational explanation. Perhaps it was a different kind of wing, or maybe the gene served another purpose in this species.

As he continued scrolling, he noticed other unusual markers.

One was a variant of the MAOA gene, linked to aggression in humans and other mammals. In this sample, the variant was quite pronounced. Whatever this creature was, it was likely capable of great violence.

Another sequence showed an abnormality in the myostatin gene that could lead to extraordinary muscle growth.

Alex sat back, his mind reeling at the implications. A creature with giant wings, immense strength, and a propensity for violence. What the hell was he looking at? A prehistoric super-predator? A mythical beast made flesh?

He glanced at the clock.

It was late, and he should head home. But how could he stop now, with such a mystery before him? He needed to analyse the sequence further, to try to make sense of these incredible findings, and in the meantime, he needed to run a second batch to verify the initial sample and rule out sample cross-contamination.

It was going to be a long night. He would need a lot more coffee, that was for sure, and some food.

Alex hurried down to the cafeteria and grabbed supplies from the vending machine, then headed back up, his mind reeling from the incredible findings.

He pushed open the door to the lab — and stopped in surprise.

Four well-built men in crisp, dark suits stood around his workbench, postures rigid, expressions severe.

One man held the printouts from the sequencing data as he scrutinised the pages with a furrowed brow. Another carefully packed the finger bone back into its insulated box.

These men were not scientists. Their bearing, their attire, everything about them screamed government agent.

A sickening sense of dread settled in Alex's stomach as the man holding the readouts looked up, his dark eyes piercing in their intensity.

"Dr Novak, is this research authorised?"

Alex opened his mouth, but no words came out. "Um... I... it's..." His mind raced for an explanation, an excuse, anything.

But under the penetrating gaze of the agent, he crumbled.

"No," he admitted, his voice barely above a whisper. "It's for a friend. But... who are you? What are you doing here?"

The agent set the papers down and walked over to Alex, standing just a fraction too close.

He was tall and well-built, with broad shoulders

that filled out his tailored suit. With Hispanic features, cropped black hair, and a defined jawline, the agent seemed the kind of guy who pumped iron at four a.m. every morning with no need to post it online to prove how hard he was.

"We're from a particular government agency with an investment in Extinct Origin. We have access to all research here, and your experiment was flagged as particularly interesting for military use."

Alex's eyes widened as he considered the implications. Incredible strength, enhanced aggression, even wings... What could a creature like that be used for? Super soldiers? Living weapons?

"The bone isn't mine," Alex protested weakly. "I don't have permission to use it for anything."

The agent narrowed his eyes. "It's our lab, Dr Novak. And this bone is in our lab. You sequenced it on our machines." He took a step even closer. "We also know about your private work. The experiments you've done that skirt ethical boundaries — and the significant debts you owe."

The agent was silent for a beat, his gaze unwavering, then he spun around and walked back to the lab bench, picking up the test results once more. "You can pack your things and leave right now. We'll take it from here."

Alex stood in shocked silence. He felt winded,

like he'd been punched in the gut. Everything he had worked for was crumbling down around him, and his future looked bleaker than ever.

After a minute, the agent looked over. "Of course, there is another option. You can work with us on this project. Help us take it to the next stage."

"You want to de-extinct it?"

The agent chuckled, a sound devoid of humour. "Of course. Why else would we be here?"

Alex exhaled slowly, knowing he had already decided. He nodded.

The agent smiled. "Good. Get some sleep, and tomorrow you'll start at a different location for classified military research. The details will be sent to your phone before dawn. You're off the thylacine project. This is your de-extinction focus now."

As the agents packed up his remaining records, Alex stood watching, his thoughts racing.

He would have to tell Emilia his research came up empty, that the bone was destroyed somehow, or he could just hand the situation over to the agent, whoever he was, to deal with.

Alex looked around the lab, at the equipment he'd used for years, the many projects he'd worked on. It all seemed different now, tainted with the knowledge of the company's military partnership.

He thought of the bone and the curious DNA

strands within. The de-extinction process couldn't possibly work on such a creature. Could it?

CHAPTER 4

EMILIA SAT UP SHARPLY, heart pounding, gasping for air.

The remnants of the nightmare clung to her mind — the monstrous creature bearing down, its powerful wings beating the air, driving a surging torrent of water that threatened to drown the world. She could almost feel the icy flood filling her lungs and her burning need for oxygen.

She reached for the familiar contours of her tent, the thin fabric rippling in the pre-dawn breeze. She was on dry land at the dig site, Göbekli Tepe. She was safe.

But the sense of unease lingered, and a clammy sheen of sweat coated her skin despite the chill of the early morning.

Emilia sat up, drawing her knees to her chest as she tried to slow her ragged breathing and calm her heartbeat.

It had been a week since the earthquake halted their excavation, and five days since she had couriered the finger bone to Professor Novak at the Boston lab, and still no word, despite her emailing multiple times.

She had rung his office repeatedly, but they fobbed her off with excuses. He was busy. He would call her back.

Perhaps he really was occupied with his company research — or perhaps she had made a terrible mistake sending her only evidence away.

Unable to bear the confines of the tent any longer, Emilia reached for her boots and jacket. She needed air. She needed to feel solid ground beneath her feet.

She stepped out into the pre-dawn light and looked over at the rubble covering the entrance to the chamber. Painstakingly excavated over months and buried within minutes of the earthquake, the pile of broken stone and dirt was now a haphazard tumble that concealed the incredible discovery beneath. The giant skeleton, the pillars with strange symbols, all buried again with currently no evidence to show of the find that could rewrite history.

A flicker of movement caught Emilia's eye, snapping her out of her dark thoughts.

An old woman knelt at the edge of the rubble, her weathered hands clasped before her. The first rays of the rising sun glinted off the silver in her hair and painted her wrinkled face in shadow. Her lips moved in silent prayer as she swayed back and forth, bowing low, almost to the ground.

Emilia frowned. It was unusual to see anyone at the site this early, let alone someone who wasn't part of the excavation team. By her clothing, the old woman wasn't a local Muslim, and it wasn't yet time for the *Fajr* dawn prayers, anyway. What was she doing here, kneeling in front of the ruined entrance as if it were a shrine?

A prickling sense of foreboding washed over Emilia like the last vestiges of the flood from her nightmare. There was something about the woman's posture, the intensity of her prayers that were unsettling. As if the old woman knew something of what lay deep beneath the earth.

The nightmare flashed through Emilia's mind once more — the beat of mighty wings, the rush of rising water.

She took a deep breath and walked over, her footsteps crunching on the debris-covered ground.

The old woman rose to her feet, her movements slow and stiff. As she turned, there was a depth to her gaze, a weight of knowledge and judgment that made Emilia's steps falter.

"*Sen hepimizin üzerine yargıyı getirdin,*" the woman said in Turkish, her voice low and grave. "You have brought judgment upon us all."

Emilia was taken aback by the woman's words. "I'm sorry. What do you mean?"

The old woman took a step closer, her weathered face etched with lines of concern. "*Devler.* The giants. If you wake them, the flood must come again."

Emilia flushed, her heart beating faster. "How do you know?"

But the old woman was already turning away, shaking her head as if in resignation.

"*İzleyiciler ve Nefilimler,*" she murmured, almost to herself. "The Watchers and the Nephilim. *Enoch'un Kitabı'nda yazıldığı gibi.* As it is written in the Book of Enoch."

Emilia tried to place the unfamiliar words. They sounded biblical, but she couldn't quite recall the context. It was a long time since her undergraduate paper on biblical archaeology.

Before she could ask any more, the old woman hurried away, her steps purposeful as she navigated the uneven terrain. She paused at the edge of the site, turning back to give Emilia one last, long look. Even from that distance, Emilia felt her judgment.

Then the old woman was gone, disappearing into the morning mist.

Emilia stood by the rubble, the woman's words playing over and over in her head, mingling with the unsettling images from her nightmare.

Giants. Floods. Judgment.

She had to know more.

She hurried across the site to the extensive library in the main building. It was more for show than serious scholarly research, but it had the best Wi-Fi.

The library was quiet and cool, and the air conditioning was a welcome respite from the growing heat outside. Emilia settled herself at a desk, plugged in her phone, and started to search online.

She began with the Nephilim and quickly found an endless array of biblical references, mythological analyses, and conspiracy theories. She scanned through them quickly, sifting useful information from overblown legend.

According to the apocryphal Book of Enoch, the Nephilim were the offspring of the 'sons of God' and the 'daughters of men.' Half human, half angelic giants who walked the earth in the days before the great flood. They were mighty warriors and men of renown, whose wickedness and violence brought the judgment of the divine upon the whole world.

The Watchers were the fallen angels who fathered the Nephilim, who taught forbidden knowledge to humanity and were punished for their sins. They were cast into darkness, bound in chains, until the day of final judgment. They wait there still.

Emilia sat back in her chair, thinking of the finger bone sitting in a lab across the ocean. Could it really belong to a Nephilim, a half-angelic biblical giant? If it were true, it would rewrite not just history, but the foundations of human belief.

Her hands shook as she scrolled through image after image of artistic renderings of Nephilim based on the scant descriptions in ancient texts. Towering figures with fierce, inhuman features, their powerful bodies rippling with unnatural strength. Great feathered wings arched from their backs, casting shadows over the human forms cowering before them.

Just like her nightmare.

The Nephilim were unstoppable by human hands, and the only way to destroy them and start again was a great Flood, like the one previously recorded in many cultures, the one that wiped out almost every life on earth.

Emilia's breath caught in her throat as the old woman's words echoed in her mind, a dire warning of judgment and cataclysm.

But it was just a myth, just a story. It had to be.

CHAPTER 5

Two years later

RACHEL RAMIREZ WALKED ALONG the dimly lit corridors of the maternity intensive care unit, her footsteps echoing off the sterile white tiles. Another night shift marked by the hum of machines and the faint, chemical scent of disinfectant mingled with the powdery smell of baby formula.

The fluorescent lights above cast a harsh, artificial glow, washing out the pale pink and blue of the walls, but at least the brightness kept her awake.

Rachel paused for a moment, leaned against the wall, and briefly closed her eyes. She was tired, so tired.

The endless shifts blurred into one another until she could hardly tell day from night, but she needed this job, so she took every overtime shift she could. Her husband had been out of work for months, laid off from the factory where he'd worked for over a decade. Without his income, they had relied on Rachel's meagre salary as a nurse in the public hospital system.

It hadn't been enough.

The bills piled up, and they'd been on the verge of losing everything when Rachel stumbled across the ad for this position. A private maternity unit with pay five times what she'd made before. It was a lifeline, a chance to keep their heads above water, and maybe even save a little.

But the job came with its own set of challenges.

Rachel didn't mind signing the stringent NDA, but she couldn't stop thinking about how the babies were so different from any she'd looked after before. These were stronger, more resilient, and they had curious bony nubs on their backs, like something growing under their skin.

She had been told not to question anything, just to make sure the children made it through each night. So she ignored the needle marks on their tiny arms and tried to push away the suspicion that these little ones were being tested all the time, maybe even experimented on.

Rachel shook her head and pushed herself off the wall, forcing her tired legs to carry her on down the corridor, back into the rhythm of the shift. She couldn't afford to let her mind wander to a darker place.

Her phone buzzed in her pocket. She pulled it out and glanced at the screen. Rising seas flooding coastal cities. Millions displaced as unusual weather patterns intensified. Another news alert, the third one in recent days, with ever more gloomy environmental headlines.

Rachel shoved her phone back in her pocket. Floods, droughts, storms of increasing intensity. The world was changing and the old certainties crumbled away. As long as there wasn't another storm surge in the Boston area, she couldn't even worry about it. She had to focus on her job and keeping her family safe and provided for. No matter what it took.

She entered the main ward for the next scheduled round of checks. The room was filled with the soft beeping of monitoring machines. Everything was as it should be.

Rachel paused at the first cot, her gaze flicking to the monitors displaying the vital signs of the infant below.

The numbers were always perfect, too perfect, but she forced herself to ignore the unease that coiled in her gut. She had to believe that everything was fine, that these babies were just babies, no matter how different they might seem.

But it was hard, because they never cried like normal infants. They didn't squirm or fuss. They hardly made a sound.

Rachel moved from cot to cot, checking the IVs that snaked into tiny veins, ensuring that the feeding tubes were secure and the monitors functioned properly.

One baby stirred across the room, his little hand escaping the swaddling blankets.

Rachel walked over, almost grateful for a moment out of the ordinary, a respite from the monotony of her shift.

She bent over the cot and gazed down at the cherubic face of the baby boy, his eyes closed as if still sleeping. She gently tucked his little arm back inside the blanket and whispered, "Who's a beautiful boy, then?"

The baby stirred.

His eyes fluttered open.

They were a startling shade of blue, so vivid and deep that for a moment, Rachel thought she glimpsed heaven in their depths.

The infant's gaze locked with hers — and Rachel's breath caught in her throat.

There was no innocence in his eyes, no hint of the blank slate of a newborn mind. Instead, there was a cold intelligence, a calculation that sent a shiver down Rachel's spine. It was the look of a predator that knew its prey had no choice but to submit.

The blue that seemed so heavenly a moment

before now held the icy glint of a frozen hell with an oncoming flood of darkness that threatened to consume the whole world.

Rachel gasped and stepped away from the cot, out of the baby's sight line.

She stood, legs trembling, hands shaking as she blinked away the vision. She was desperate to run, to get out of this place and never return… but she needed this job.

Rachel took a deep breath. *Come on now, get it together. These are just little babies.*

She was tired, under-caffeinated. It was just some kind of weird hallucination. There was nothing wrong here, nothing wrong at all.

AUTHOR'S NOTE

Living systems are never in equilibrium. They are inherently unstable. They may seem stable, but they're not. Everything is moving and changing. In a sense, everything is on the edge of collapse.

—Michael Crichton, *Jurassic Park*

Back in July 1993, I went to see *Jurassic Park* on its opening weekend in Bristol, UK. I was eighteen, and on a first date.

We hadn't booked so by the time we got to the front of the queue, there were only single tickets left. My date suggested we do something else, but I really wanted to see the movie, so we bought separate tickets and watched it several rows away from each other.

I loved it, and I've seen the original several times in the years since, along with all the other Jurassic Park franchise films. I also love Michael Crichton's thrillers, and of course, the book is better than the film!

Thirty years later, in 2023, I heard Ben Lamm, the CEO of Colossal Laboratories & Biosciences, talk about de-extinction in a podcast interview, where he described his mission to 'de-extinct' woolly mammoths and the thylacine.

This idea fascinated me, but it inspired other thriller authors too, and I didn't want to write something similar. Check out *The Great Zoo of China* by Matthew Reilly, *The Bone Labyrinth* by James Rollins, or *Extinction* by Douglas Preston, all fantastic thrillers.

Then I discovered that the CIA invested in Colossal under their In-Q-Tel nonprofit investment arm, aiming to "weave biology and technology into the DNA of national security." They note, "It's less about the mammoths and more about the capability."

I knew I had to write a story, but with a J.F. Penn spin toward biblical archaeology. I've always found the Nephilim fascinating, so I decided their de-extinction might be an interesting development. But where might their bones be found?

Göbekli Tepe is a fascinating prehistoric site built over 11,000 years ago, over six thousand years before Stonehenge. There are twenty circular stone enclosures, and some of the pillars weigh up to ten tons. While there are mysterious symbols and figures, the tomb of the Nephilim is my invention. Unless, of course, they just haven't found it yet...

Related links

"An immense mystery older than Stonehenge," BBC Travel, accessed 18 April 2024 — www.bbc.com/travel/article/20210815-an-immense-mystery-older-than-stonehenge

Colossal Laboratories & Biosciences — www.colossal.com

"How AI is helping solve extinction." *Moonshots and Mindsets* podcast with Peter Diamandis — www.diamandis.com/podcast/ben-lamm

Jurassic Park — Michael Crichton

"Mammoth Interest: The CIA Invests in Dallas-Based Colossal Biosciences," Dallas Innovates, accessed 18 April 2024 — dallasinnovates.com/mammoth-interest-the-cia-invests-in-dallas-based-colossal-biosciences/

WITH A
DEMON'S EYE

If you gaze long enough into an abyss,
the abyss will gaze back into you.

—Friedrich Nietzsche

THE DESERT SHIMMERED IN the heat as the sun beat down, punishing a land that had seen over a thousand years of suffering with no end in sight.

Sara Miles stared out from the back of the Humvee, her legs cramped from sitting for hours on end. The heat of the desert was like a furnace blast, even through the protective window glass. Her lips were cracked and peeling, the back of her neck blistered from months embedded with the military battalion.

She gripped her camera more tightly, anchoring herself as images from yesterday's mission resurfaced, like a twisted mirage over the sand.

Snapshots of bodies in the rubble. What had once been a family reduced to mangled corpses covered in dust and ash.

Another drone strike. More collateral damage in a never-ending war.

On her first tour, Sara had found it hard to capture the brutality and destruction, her breath catching in her throat, her tears obscuring the viewfinder as she tried to focus. Now her pictures were crisp and clear, the images telling a deliberate story, her sentiment locked deep inside where it couldn't cloud her vision.

Mags leaned over from the front passenger seat, holding out a wrapped mint sweet in his out-stretched fingers. "Want one?"

For an officer in the Medical Corps, in charge of other people's health, Mags sure had a sweet tooth.

Sara shook her head.

Mags always offered. She always declined. The comfort of a familiar routine, perhaps even more precious so far from home.

Their patrol was heading for an encampment on the far reaches of the territory. The military provided the settlers with essential supplies, and the people had proved friendly, but were understandably cautious. Today they were delivering medical supplies and food rations — and hopefully returning with a little more good will. Sara had jumped at the chance to join Mags and Harvey, their driver, on the run north, hoping to take photos of something other than misery.

Even with the faltering air-con in the Humvee, it was still unbearably hot and the vehicle stank of stale sweat. Sara opened the window for a fraction of fresh air, but it only let in a wave of heat and dust. A bead of sweat trickled down her back, pooling at the base of her spine.

It was impossible to stay dry and clean out here in this land of blood and dust, but when she returned to the sterilised world of her London flat, where she could be freshly showered and sweet smelling, Sara missed the desert with every fibre of her being. This was real life, and what she did as a combat photographer mattered.

She was nothing in the bustling city — but out here in the desert, she captured the truth of war. Her photos shone a light on those who fought, suffered, and died for their freedom, for their country, and for their family. Some were soldiers, some were civilians. All were caught up in a maelstrom beyond their control.

Her images could sway public perception and damn a government to hell for their actions. Once, she had even managed to quiet the drones — at least for a few days. But war had its own impetus, and its hunger was not assuaged here.

A boyfriend — one of the many who passed briefly through Sara's life — once told her she was incapable of seeing anything without the lens of war, that she would only find true happiness if she put her camera aside and experienced the world without the frame of the viewfinder.

That day, she had picked up her camera and walked out of his life. She would be nothing without the ability to see the truth of the world through her lens. If that meant living alone, then so be it.

The desert terrain soon gave way to rocky hills, and the Humvee turned in a wide arc to head along a rutted road on the final approach to the encampment.

Its location at the crossroads of a trade route was strategic, so the place had been torn between all sides in the conflict, wrenched back and forth until it was left broken and bloody.

Factions had shelled the village, uprooting its people and leaving them homeless refugees. But again and again, they returned and rebuilt, uncovering ancient foundations and using broken bricks from one generation to provide shelter for the next. Tin-roofed homes were cobbled together from salvaged military equipment reinforced with old tires, bent rebar, and planks of reclaimed wood.

The makeshift shelters might be shattered and fragmented, but Sara knew she would find beauty here through the prism of her lens. The shy sideways glance of a young woman in the shadows, the wrinkled face of an old man, the broad grin of a child unbowed by suffering. Her images could change the perspective of those who saw them, and this bombed-out encampment might yet become a beacon of hope, a story of survival, one that drew international aid and a level of protection for this community.

The Humvee jerked from side to side on the rocky surface, and Harvey slowed the vehicle to a crawl on the uneven road.

"This is worse than usual." He shook his head as he gripped the steering wheel more tightly. "We have to get some engineers out here before it gets any worse or we'll never get through next time."

Two little boys, both around nine years old, ran out from the village and jogged alongside the Humvee, their hands thrust out for sweets.

"Hello, please," one shouted, a wide smile on his face, his dark eyes expectant.

Sara wound down the window and raised her camera, capturing his cheeky grin and long limbs against the backdrop of the desert. The boy ran in bare feet over the rocky surface with the ease of one who belonged to this land. Sara could only hope her image captured this carefree moment, a boy in his element, as it should be.

As Harvey tried to rev the Humvee forward, the gears ground together with a metallic rasp and the engine stalled and died. They were only a few hundred meters from the village.

"Damn it, there are too many rocks." Harvey nodded at Mags. "Clear some away from the front wheels and I'll try again."

Mags opened the door and stepped out into the heat of the desert sun.

The two boys ran up and tugged at his uniform.

"Please, thank you," they giggled with the few English words they'd learned.

Mags reached into his pocket, and Sara captured his generous smile with a snapshot, the desert dust pale against his black skin as he reached out with the last of his mint sweets.

Through her lens, she caught two hands briefly touching — the man and the boy, the soldier and the war-torn child, the invader and the oppressed.

A sudden flash of magnesium white.

A crack and a roar. A blast of hot air.

The wrenching sound of metal as the Humvee bucked and rolled.

The blast crushed Sara's chest and tore the breath from her lungs. Her vision faded and her ears rang as smoke billowed around the half-exploded vehicle. She gasped for breath, inhaling the stench of burnt flesh and hot metal, coughing and retching as she fought to escape.

A blistering heat flashed across her skin as she crawled her way out onto the burning sand. Sara screwed her eyes shut against the flames and smoke, and although she couldn't see anything, that last moment remained seared into her memory.

Mags. The children.

Perhaps they were injured. Perhaps she could help. She just had to find them.

Sara wiped her eyes with the back of one hand, trying to clear her vision.

Sparks of such intense pain shot through her skull that she doubled over with a wave of nausea.

After a moment, she touched her eyes more gently with light fingertips. There were shards of glass embedded in her face.

In her eyes.

Another sudden blinding flash of light.

The boom that followed was like thunder, the detonation echoing across the desert as fresh blood joined that of generations past under the sand.

*   *   *

Three days later

Sara lay in a hospital ward at a military medical centre, bandages over her eyes. The room smelled of antiseptic, but it couldn't mask the stink of pus and blood from her wounds, the stench of burned flesh and hot metal and charred sand. She knew these were sensory memories — a nurse had told her so during her first panic attack — but she still had to fight them back.

Sara clutched the edge of the bed as she anchored herself to the physical world.

Inhale for three.

Exhale for three.

Once she had calmed her racing heart, Sara reached up and gently felt around the side of her facial bandages. There was a distinct pain where the edges of her raw nerves still functioned. But behind her eyes, there was only a throbbing deep within her skull.

She was lucky, they said. The explosion had killed both soldiers and one of the children. She had been badly injured, but she would make it.

They gave her drugs for the pain, drugs for the panic, drugs for sleep.

Each had their own colour. White, blue, red, red, red. Lights flashed in her imagined vision, at once both bright and dark, like parts of the sky fallen to earth with the rain of shrapnel and glass.

She was lucky, they said, but Sara wished that what was left of Mags would rise up and drag her beneath the sand. She wished his blood would choke her, and the scuttling insects of the desert would burrow into her bleeding eye sockets to devour what was left of her broken body.

The door creaked, and footsteps approached her bed.

"Morning, Sara, I'm Doctor Hasabi. I'm in charge of the experimental treatment program here at Westfield Military. How are you feeling today?"

His tone was brusque, matter-of-fact. He must have seen much worse than her in this bed, and Sara was grateful for his lack of pity.

She turned her bandaged face toward him. "As good as can be expected."

She paused, but she had to ask. It was the only thing she cared about now. "Will I get my sight back?"

The scrape of a metal chair on tile. A shift in the air by her bedside as the doctor sat down.

The shuffle of papers. The scent of spearmint as if the doctor had been chewing gum, or swilling mouthwash.

Sara pushed the thought of Mags and his mint sweets away as Doctor Hasabi spoke.

"Your eyes were severely damaged in the explosion. We removed the glass and metal shards, but we cannot restore your sight. The damage is too great."

The doctor's voice faded away as the pounding in her head grew louder. Sara struggled for breath as his words lay heavy on her chest, crushing her spark of hope to dust.

He touched her hand. "Sara, it's okay. Take some deep breaths. There is a possibility you could see again, at least partially, but there are risks."

His words echoed in her mind, coalescing into a way out of the interminable darkness.

"What… what do you mean?"

"We have a new eye transplant program using eyes that are part human, part robotic. It's experimental, both in terms of the technology and the procedure. We have to connect the vasculature, the blood supply, and musculature so you can move the eye, and then rewire the pathway to your optic nerve. It's essentially brain surgery, so it is extremely high risk—"

"I'll do it." Sara cut him off. "I'm a photographer. Without my sight, I cannot do my job."

My job is my life. I am nothing without it.

The click of a pen top and the sound of writing on paper.

Sara could almost hear the doctor thinking. Was she a suitable candidate for the surgery? Was she stable enough?

Inhale for three.

Exhale for three.

Repeat.

The wait seemed endless as the doctor weighed her life in the balance.

Finally, he spoke. "I have to read you the waiver form since you can't read it yourself. It's long, but we have to cover all eventualities and then you can make your final decision. I'll record your verbal consent in addition to signing the forms."

Doctor Hasabi read the pages, his tone blurring into monotony as Sara listened to the litany of potential dangers — visual distortions, chronic pain, brain damage, death — and responded in the affirmative to every possible dire scenario.

They finally reached the end. "Knowing the risks, do you consent to the surgery?"

"Yes, absolutely. As soon as possible."

"Sign here." The doctor pushed a clipboard under Sara's hand and guided her to the right spot.

She scrawled her signature.

The chair grated on the tiles once more as Doctor Hasabi stood up. "We can proceed this afternoon. The nurse will be in to prep you for surgery shortly."

The door creaked shut once more and Sara lay in the bed, the beep of medical machines keeping a pulse with her heart, as she clung to the hope of seeing once more.

It wasn't long until a nurse came in, all speed and efficiency.

The squeeze of a blood pressure cuff.

The prick of a needle for blood draws.

The sound of rubber wheels on vinyl as she was wheeled to the operating theatre.

Sara imagined the place in snapshots as sounds conjured the hospital corridors around her. Someone — a nurse, perhaps — walked past, footsteps faltering in the hallway as they stared down, wondering what horrors lay beneath the bandages. A deep voice called for help from a nearby room, a sound of desperation as a loved one passed beyond reach of the living.

Once within the operating theatre, capable hands transferred her from the gurney to the table.

It was freezing cold and a thin blanket did little to warm her. Sara shifted on the table, her gown rustling as the sounds of preparation went on around her. There was a sense of anticipation in the air, a barely restrained excitement at the experimental procedure ahead.

As the last minutes ticked by before she went under anaesthetic, Sara considered what might happen next. What remained of her eyes gouged out of her head, left like jelly in a metal tray. A blade in her brain. The smell of burning.

What if they cut too deep? What if she woke up with more deficits than she already had? What if the pain was too much?

But the alternative was to never see again, never look through the lens of her camera and show the world a snapshot of the truth.

Doctor Hasabi leaned over the table. "We just need to do some last checks while you're awake, but it won't take long. Try to relax."

As he gently unwrapped the bandages around her face, Sara felt a chill touch her exposed skin and the gaze of the operating theatre upon her.

A gasp came from across the room, swiftly silenced.

Cool fingers on her cheeks, fitting a mask over her mouth and nose.

"Just relax, breathe easily now."

As the world faded to black, Sara saw Mags reaching for her from the desert sand. Where his eyes should be were burning, bloody holes.

*   *   *

Sara woke screaming.

Intense pain split her skull, as if the neurons in her brain were being rewired with blades and flame.

She clutched at her head, clawing at the bandages, whimpering in agony. She tried to open her eyes, but they were welded shut, crusted over with the residue of burned cells and stitches and blood. The horror of it crashed over her like a wave.

Alarms blared. A nurse rushed in.

The prick of a needle brought the relief of blackness once more.

*   *   *

When she woke again, something had changed, as if the rewiring was complete. The pain was a dull ache under the gentle fog of whatever drugs they'd given her.

A breath from beside her bed and the swish of a medical gown.

"Sara, it's Doctor Hasabi — just relax. I'm going to remove the bandages and examine you."

His fingertips were cool, and Sara wondered how deep into her skull they had probed.

"I'm going to shine a light into your right eye now."

Sara gasped. "I see something."

"Good, good. Blink for me."

Sara blinked, her eyelids fluttering as the doctor's face emerged slowly from the haze. It was blurred, but still, she could see him.

Hope almost burst from her chest at the sheer relief. She would see again. She would go back to the desert. She would get her life back.

"Keep blinking. Let the eye adjust."

As the doctor stepped away, Sara saw his features more clearly.

A portly Middle Eastern man with a hawk-like nose and a proud smile that welcomed her back to the world while appreciating his own skill as a surgeon.

But there was something around him, a blurred shape, like a shadow crawling over his back. Something like claws dug into the doctor's skull; something with articulated joints and a bony carapace clung to him.

Sara blinked once more, trying to clear the strange vision as Doctor Hasabi looked down at his notes.

"There's a minuscule piece of shrapnel from the explosion still embedded at the very back of your eye. It's too dangerous to remove, so there is a risk it will dislodge at some point. But we can monitor that with follow-up scans."

Sara imagined his words in a visual snapshot. A piece of grey metal surrounded by the red of her veins. A speck of war and violence embedded in her brain, soaked in the blood of the dead.

Strangely, it comforted her to think of carrying it with her as a reminder of those lost.

Doctor Hasabi held up a chart of letters and numbers.

"Can you read this line?"

As Sara passed each of the visual tests, she wondered how soon she could get back out to the desert, how fast she could embed herself back with the military. Surely her scars and her resilience made her even more suited to that life. Her job was war, and while humans walked the earth, there would always be work for such as her.

Doctor Hasabi nodded as he lowered the charts. "As far as I can tell, your vision is already much better than I would expect, and it will only improve. But what do you think? Do you have any distortions or auras in your field of vision?"

As the doctor spoke, the shadowy creature crawled out from behind him, its grotesque claws digging into his flesh, its black eyes staring at her with what she thought was recognition.

Sara opened her mouth to tell the doctor what she saw. Perhaps he could go back in, remove that piece of shrapnel, and fix the visual distortion. For surely that's all it was?

Or perhaps the fragment of metal stained with the blood of sacrifice enabled her to see a demon of violence. None were innocent in the theatre of war, not even the surgeon who stitched up the wounded.

Perhaps this new vision would help her identify the darkness that hid within the hearts of those she photographed. The demons of war would never be exorcised from the world, and it was her job to take photos of what kept them alive.

"Everything looks perfect. I don't see any distortions."

The doctor nodded and wrote on his chart. "Okay, I'll be back to check on you later."

Sara reached out and touched his sleeve. "Thank

you, doctor, but before you go, can I see what I look like? I know there will be scars, but I want to see. Please?"

After a moment's hesitation, Doctor Hasabi reached into his pocket. "I would prefer to wait, but since you asked."

He pulled out a small mirror and handed it to her.

At first, Sara could only see the inflamed criss-cross patchwork of scars across her face, marring her skin with lines of stitches and purple bruising. Her left eyelid was sewn closed to hide the trauma beneath although the doctor had said they might be able to fix it with a later surgery. Her right eye was no longer hazel, but a strange vibrant blue — so different from her natural colour, but somehow perfectly right for her new face.

Then the creature crawled out from behind her back.

It had leathery skin, the shade of diseased fungus growing on a corpse. Its flesh was stretched tight over a skeletal frame, and it had a distorted skull with clouded, sightless eyes and long limbs that wrapped around her like a second skin.

Sara gasped at the vision, biting her lip as she stared into the blank eyes of the demon, a promise of bloodshed and battle in its expression.

Doctor Hasabi patted her arm. "I know the scars are shocking, but they will heal in time and there's the possibility of plastic surgery for the worst of it. Your sight is the focus for now. Are you sure your vision is clear?"

Sara looked up at him. "Yes, doctor. I can see perfectly now. Perhaps even better than before."

AUTHOR'S NOTE

I've been severely short-sighted since I was eleven and wore glasses and then contact lenses for most of my adult life. A few years ago, I had laser eye surgery, which was amazing and definitely changed my life for the better.

But it's a weird and slightly disturbing operation!

There is a short period of time when you lie on a gurney and look up into a bright light. There's a smell of cells burning away and if you think too hard about it, you realise that a machine is lasering your eyeball.

So you breathe and concentrate on staying calm, and then it's over so quickly. The operation didn't hurt at all, although there was about 48 hours of pain afterwards.

A few days later, you can see properly.

Having that operation was one of the best choices I have made, and I appreciate my eyesight every day.

It's amazing what we will do to keep our eyesight — and I wondered how far I would go, especially in an era of brain implants and technology that could help people with impairments.

How far would you go?

* * *

As I thought about who would have the most to lose when it came to their sight, I read a memoir by a combat photographer: *It's What I Do: A Photographer's Life of Love and War* by Lynsey Addario.

It's a great book and demonstrates why photographers take such risks and what they love about the job.

* * *

Many of my stories have aspects of demonology in them, and this one brought to mind a scene in *Delirium* when Blake Daniel returns home only to find demons feasting on his dying father.

I think it was my teenage years of reading supernatural warfare books like *Running with the Demon* by Terry Brooks. I just can't help myself writing them!

SEAHENGE

We are the children of the flood. All of us living today are descended from those who saw their lands drowned, civilisations crumble and populations scatter. Floods linger deep in our cultural memory, when an old world died in violence, and a new one was born.

—Gareth E. Rees, *Sunken Lands: A Journey Through Flooded Kingdoms and Lost Worlds*

CHAPTER 1

THE NORTH SEA CHURNED along the Norfolk coast, a vast cauldron of slate-grey water whipped to a frenzy by the howling wind. An advancing wall of charcoal cloud shot through with lightning bolts smothered the last rays of early sunlight as gulls wheeled, fleeing inland, their cries lost in the rising wind.

The first droplets of rain fell on one lonely beach, the pattering sound intensifying as the deluge arrived, blurring the line between sea and sky.

Waves crashed against the shore of the ancient fens as the storm surge pushed relentlessly inland. It flooded the coastal marshes, swirling through strands of sea lavender and salt-marsh grass, uprooting the plants that held the dunes together. As each wave receded, it took with it another fistful of the land.

Eventually, the storm ebbed, and the rain slackened to a steady drizzle, revealing the extent of the damage.

The coastline had been reshaped. Where there had been dunes, there were now only jagged cuts into the land. The beach, usually a gentle slope, was now a chaos of debris and newly carved channels of water running back to the sea.

And there, emerging from the receding tide, a perfect circle of tall timber spars. The wood was dark, almost black, preserved by long immersion in peat and sand. The spars glistened in the weak morning light, still slick with sea water and strands of seaweed. As the light shifted, it cast shadows along the wood, illuminating marks of ancient tools and ritual symbols in a long-lost language.

At the centre of the circle, a massive tree stump stood inverted, its gnarled roots reaching for the sky, forming a central platform. In its twisted embrace lay the remains of something long forgotten.

A flock of gulls, returning now the storm had passed, wheeled overhead but did not approach. Their cries seemed muted, distant, as if they called across a vast gulf of time.

CHAPTER 2

THE WIND WHIPPED STRANDS of Dr Evelyn
Price's grey hair across her face as she stepped out
of her Land Rover later that day. She pushed the
errant strands into her beanie hat and rubbed her
hands together against the cold as she looked down
onto the beach.

The Norfolk coast stretched out before her with
the aftermath of last night's storm etched into the
landscape, the dunes forever reshaped. But it was
the perfect circle of dark wooden spars emerging
from the shallow water on the beach that drew her
attention.

It was clearly Neolithic — similar timber circles
had been discovered from that time — but this
was different. The inverted tree stump at its centre
was unusual, but what lay upon it might be even
more so. A tarpaulin covered the central section to
protect what lay beneath, and she was keen to get
down there to examine it.

The call had come a few hours ago from the
local police requesting Evelyn's team take over the
investigation at this newly emerged site. While
remains had been found, the initial police forensic

assessment had determined them to be historic. Evelyn was Head of Maritime Archaeology at Historic England and although her team was presently engaged with a shipwreck in the Thames Estuary, she could already see that this site would take precedence.

Evelyn hurried down the dunes, her boots sinking into the wet sand as she made her way along the beach. It smelled of brine and the rot of sea creatures churned up and scattered across the shore. The cries of gulls pierced the air as they scavenged the wreckage.

As Evelyn approached the excavation site, she recognised Dr Marcus Holbrook, an archaeologist and director of a local museum. They had worked together in the past, and she appreciated his meticulous approach. A team of archaeological workers bustled around him, shoring up the newly emerged structure to protect it from the elements before the tide rose once more.

"Over here, Evelyn!" Marcus waved her over, his silver hair plastered to his forehead from sea spray, his windbreaker doing little to protect him from the elements.

Evelyn walked through the outer ring of staves. There were over fifty standing close together, forming a kind of enclosure within, and she noticed tool marks in the dark wood arranged in ritual patterns. Spirals, circles, horizontal marks, and zigzag lines. Perhaps a map of the heavens or prayers to an ancient sea god.

Marcus pointed to the tarpaulin-covered central stump. "It's extraordinary. I've never seen anything like it." He gestured to a set of stones, placed as steps next to the covered platform. "We have to move it soon or it's going to disintegrate from exposure."

He stood back, biting his lip in anticipation of her reaction. Evelyn had never seen the usually mild-mannered director so intensely excited by a discovery.

She used the stones to step up and carefully lifted one corner of the tarpaulin from around the gnarled edges of the ancient roots of the upturned tree.

The body, clearly a woman, was impossibly old, yet preserved in the peat, her skin leathery and darkened to a deep mahogany. She lay cradled by the root structure, cupped by the base of the ancient tree.

Dark, tangled strands of hair, matted with peat, clung to her scalp. The skin of her face was drawn tight, lips pulled back over what looked like sharpened teeth. Her hollowed eye sockets stared out from beneath what remained of a fragile brow, the skin stretched so thin it seemed barely more than a film over bone.

Her arms and torso were withered but whole, the sinew and skin preserved in the oxygen-starved environment, giving the body an almost waxen appearance. Faint tattoos or ritual markings were etched into her skin, the symbols barely visible on the peat-stained flesh.

Evelyn shifted slightly, leaning over to view more of the body — and gasped at what she saw.

The creature had no legs, but instead, a long powerful tail of smooth, leathery skin that tapered into a delicate fin with faint scales still visible. The tail curled in and out of the roots, as though the tree had grown around the body, holding it in a final embrace.

Evelyn frowned as she tried to make sense of it. Was this a hybrid sacrifice, with parts fused after death? Fake mermaids persisted in various cultures, with the most famous being P. T. Barnum's Fiji mermaid, constructed from the torso and head of a monkey sewn onto the back half of a fish. Perhaps the Neolithic people who lived here had made such a creature to honour their sea god?

Evelyn stood on her tiptoes to see even closer, careful not to touch the wood or the remains, but desperate to make out whether the join was obvious. But the transition from human to fish was seamless, at least from what she could see.

She stepped back down onto the sand, her mind reeling.

Marcus couldn't contain his excitement. "What do you think? Is it real?"

Evelyn took a deep breath of the chill, briny air and shook her head. "I don't know, but we have to act fast to preserve the site and the remains. Only once it's back in the lab under controlled conditions can we investigate any further."

A wave crashed onto the wooden spars, sending a spray of saltwater over the site. "We don't have much time. Let's get to work."

The next few hours were a blur of activity. Evelyn directed her team with practiced efficiency, setting up barriers to direct the tide around the site while they documented everything step by step.

One of the environmental archaeologists knelt in the sand, carefully extracting core samples from around the timbers and then sampling the posts themselves, meticulously scraping minute amounts of wood and sediment into labelled vials.

Evelyn turned to Marcus. "How deep do you think the posts go?"

Marcus shrugged. "Hard to say without ground-penetrating radar but given their height above ground and the preservation state, at least a meter, maybe more."

"I agree." She sighed. "It's going to take too long to get them all out at once. We'll have to do it in stages, as the tide allows."

A buzz came from behind them as Samuel Chen, their resident tech expert, launched a drone with a high-resolution camera to map a detailed 3D model of the site.

Within minutes, Samuel called out with excitement. "Evelyn! You need to see this."

Evelyn hurried over to check his laptop screen, where a preliminary model of the site rendered slowly. Samuel pointed to the marks on the timbers that she had noticed on first approaching the site. The camera angles highlighted them, and specialised filters enhanced the images even more.

"These patterns aren't random. They're a language of sorts. I'll need to adapt my custom model, but perhaps we'll be able to translate at least some of it."

Evelyn grinned, sharing his excitement. Such a find made this site even more valuable. "Good catch. Make sure you get detailed scans of every timber, and we can examine them all further back at the lab."

As she turned back to the central upturned tree, a gust of wind made her gasp with its intensity. Dark clouds gathered once more on the horizon.

"Weather's turning!" she shouted to her team.

"Let's secure the remains as a priority and try to get at least one of those timber spars out. We'll have to come back again tomorrow for the next batch."

As the wind drove the dark clouds closer and closer, her team raced to protect the remains. Their specialist truck arrived with tanks designed to keep specimens in the damp conditions they were used to before the preservation process began. As it backed down the beach with its custom lift attached, Evelyn supervised her team as they prepared to move the remains.

They worked with painstaking care, using soft brushes to remove as much sand and debris as possible before applying a consolidant to stabilise the fragile flesh, but there was no easy way to remove it from the upturned roots.

Evelyn sighed. "We're going to have to cut the wood closest to the body. It's better to damage a little of the tree than risk the remains."

One of her technicians carefully cut through several of the upturned roots with a small electric saw until the creature could be wrapped, ready for lifting.

Two team members supervised a specially designed cradle, custom-built for delicate remains, as it swung from the truck down to the creature. They attached it around the body and the entangled roots.

Evelyn could scarcely breathe as the team looked to her for the command to lift. She hated to disturb the archaeological scene, but they couldn't leave the creature here. With the storm returning, it might be gone by morning or destroyed by the elements. They had to take the risk.

"On three," she called out. "One... two... three!"

The cradle lifted. The creature rose from its rooted grave.

A sickening crack rang out.

The central tree stump split open, dark oily sediment seeping from its core. A fissure opened in the sand beneath it, running like a jagged scar towards the sea.

"Stop! Stop!" Evelyn shouted, her heart pounding. "Everyone, step back."

The team retreated, watching in silence as the crack in the sand widened. Water bubbled up from beneath, dark and frothing, come to reclaim what it had lost.

"That's not good," Marcus muttered.

Evelyn's mind raced. The structural integrity of the entire site could be compromised. They needed to move fast, but safely. Take as much as they could now, and hope that the spars were still here tomorrow.

Once the crack stopped growing, the team moved with renewed urgency.

They lifted the remains with no further damage, carefully transferring the creature to a special container filled with preservation fluid in the truck, before using the crane to remove one of the timber spars.

As the truck drove off with its precious cargo, Evelyn stood looking out over the beach once more. The wind was getting up again and dark clouds swelled overhead, threatening more heavy rain.

The tide churned around the enclosure they had built to protect the timber circle. It held for now, but it wouldn't stop the violence of another storm. Luckily, the weather was due to hold at least a little longer, and Evelyn was determined to retrieve all the spars as well as the central stump in the coming days.

As she turned to go, she glimpsed something out in the rising waves — a vast shadow lurking just beneath the water.

The hairs rose on the back of her neck, and she shuddered with a primal fear she had only felt once before.

Years ago, she had been down in a submarine, part of an expedition to the deep sea drop-off of the Porcupine Abyssal Plain, a vast stretch of ocean floor off the south-west coast of Ireland, which plunged to depths of over four thousand metres.

The memory surged back. The darkness of the abyss where light could not penetrate. Immense pressure all around her and the bitter chill biting through the hull of the submarine. The deep was no place for humans and down there Evelyn had the sense of being watched by something vast and ancient. Something that did not tolerate trespass in its domain.

She shook her head, pushing away the memory as she headed back to her car. It must only be the shadows of the clouds on the waves.

CHAPTER 3

SAMUEL CHEN'S FINGERS FLEW across the keyboard as he task-switched between three large monitors. The lab hummed with the sound of climate-controlled storage units and outside, the storm that battered the coast yesterday had passed, leaving behind a grey, listless sky. Perfect weather for coding.

On his right-hand screen, a 3D model of the Seahenge site rotated slowly. Each timber was rendered in exquisite detail, a composite from the high-definition drone footage combined with detailed photos from the scene.

Samuel zoomed in on one post and examined the intricate spirals and complex geometric patterns.

"What do you mean?" he murmured, adjusting his glasses.

He glanced over at the large tank across the lab where the creature — the 'mermaid,' as the team had started calling her — floated in a carefully balanced preservation solution. Even from this distance, he could make out the unsettling merger of human and fish.

Two bio-archaeologists pored through scans of

the creature, trying to figure out a way they could work on the remains without damaging them. They seemed determined to prove she was a hoax, but Samuel remained open-minded. Merfolk existed in the myths and stories of most cultures, so who's to say they were not real at some point? They might still roam the deep, hidden from the destructive influence of man.

Perhaps Seahenge was a sky burial for one of their kind. Many ancient cultures practiced it — the Tibetans, some Native American tribes, and the Zoroastrians with their Towers of Silence. The body was exposed to the elements and scavenging birds, who returned the dead to the circle of nature.

Samuel refocused on his own task, pulling up a database of Neolithic symbols from sites across Britain and Europe. Stonehenge, Avebury, Newgrange — he'd studied them all. But this was different, which made it such a worthy challenge.

"Okay, let's try something new." He stretched and cracked his knuckles before opening a custom-built artificial intelligence program he had developed. It was designed to analyse patterns and suggest possible meanings based on a vast corpus of ancient symbols and linguistic structures.

He'd trained it on everything from Sumerian cuneiform to Linear B, from Egyptian hieroglyphs to Norse runes, and even fed it conspiracy theories about advanced civilisations before our own, and drowned cities like the mythical Atlantis. Some might frown on that kind of data as unscientific, but all myths had a grain of ancient truth.

As the program processed the Seahenge symbols, Samuel leaned back in his chair, considering the other Neolithic sites he'd studied.

Woodhenge came to mind — another timber circle, though much larger than Seahenge. Six concentric rings of posts, possibly roofed, creating a vast structure. But Woodhenge had been on dry land, far from the sea. What made the builders of Seahenge choose such a precarious location?

Then there was the Sanctuary near Avebury, a complex of timber circles later replaced by stone. The way the posts had been arranged suggested astronomical alignments, a common feature in many Neolithic structures.

Samuel checked the status of the first run.

The model was making progress, identifying repeating patterns and potential phonetic values. He fine-tuned some parameters, guiding the machine-learning algorithm to explore specific linguistic possibilities.

He went to make some coffee, and on his return, a soft chime indicated the initial analysis was complete. Samuel leaned in, eager to explore the findings.

But the results were a disappointment.

The model had identified several recurring patterns, and drawn connections to early proto-writing systems, but meaning remained elusive.

Samuel sighed, but it was a little too much to expect answers on the first run.

The sound of heavy machinery and raised voices pulled him from his chair to the window.

Outside, in the facility's loading bay, Evelyn directed the team as they unloaded more of the massive timbers from the truck. As they lifted one of the spars, the light caught a section of wood that had been below the sand.

There were more symbols down there. Symbols that Samuel's model was missing. Perhaps they would provide the data needed to crack the code.

He grabbed his camera and scanning equipment and hurried out of the lab, heading down to the loading bay.

Evelyn stood amidst her team, directing the movement of the huge timbers.

"Careful now!" she shouted as the crane lowered another spar into place.

Samuel walked over. "How many do we have now?"

Evelyn turned, exhaustion etched on her face. "Forty so far. Only fifteen left on the beach, plus that damned central stump. The crack has widened and we're racing the tide and the weather, but I think we'll have them all by the end of tomorrow."

Samuel updated her on his progress with analysing the markings. "I think the problem might be missing data. That last spar you brought in has etched symbols below the level I scanned before."

"Makes sense," Evelyn said. "The henge was not originally built on the water, but on the edge, so the sand-line wouldn't have been so deep originally. You should be able to get pictures from most of them now, though. Go on through."

Evelyn waved him away and returned to directing the crew, while Samuel walked on into the cavernous preservation area. It was designed to accommodate large maritime artefacts and Samuel had even seen the hulls of ancient ships in here, but the space was now dwarfed by the size and number of the Seahenge timbers.

Each lay on specially designed cradles, their surfaces wrapped in thick polyethylene sheeting, which helped to retain moisture. Underneath, wet hessian cloths soaked in saltwater were wrapped tightly around the wood, keeping the timbers from drying out. Without constant care, the delicate balance of moisture within the timbers could shift, causing them to crack or deteriorate as the water-logged fibres dried out too quickly.

The entire area smelled of brine, the scent hanging in the cool air as if the sea itself lingered here, refusing to let go of its ancient relics.

Samuel approached the nearest timber and peeled back the hessian cloth around the end so he could examine the surface. The dark wood was a maze of patterned grain and symbolic marks.

He looked around the vast hall. Given the way each timber was positioned, with the protective wrapping clinging to much of their surfaces, he wouldn't be able to photograph all sides of every post, and it would take time to get even what he could.

But he had to try.

Samuel called in some of the lab techs to help the process go faster, and together, they circled the spars, taking photos from every angle.

Their footsteps echoed through the hall, mingling with the steady drip of water from the soaked cloths that still clung to the wood. The flash of each shot briefly illuminated the deep grain of the timbers, revealing details of the ancient tool marks etched into the dark surface.

As the hours passed, more spars arrived, until

Evelyn finally called a halt for the day. "Thanks, everyone. There's only the main stump left. We'll extract it tomorrow. Get some sleep now."

Samuel let the lab techs head off home while he finished up with the photos of the final spars.

When everyone had gone, he stood in the stillness of the vast hall, alone with the ancient timbers. He inhaled, breathing in the salt air as a sense of reverence rose within. These pillars had together been a sacred site and as Samuel stood before them, he felt the weight of history upon him.

He was one of the first to see the collection of spars in their entirety in perhaps four thousand years. It was impossible to comprehend such a great span of time, but the ocean waves had crashed onto the shore then as they did now. How insignificant he was on the face of the earth and how brief his time here when measured against the vast arc of history.

Samuel pushed away the thoughts of mortality. If he could decipher the symbols, he might just secure a legacy that lived on after him.

But to do that, he needed more photos.

It was almost one o'clock in the morning when he finally finished loading up the photos to his model. As the system began its analysis, the 3D image of Seahenge on his computer transformed. It had been impressive but incomplete, and now it shifted, becoming a complex pattern of interlocking symbols and patterns that grew more intricate as each photo loaded.

Samuel couldn't help but grin with excitement. This would reveal something important. He knew it. It would just take a little more time.

He looked at his watch. The team would start early on extracting the central stump once the tide was out far enough, and he wanted to have an update for Evelyn by the time she arrived.

Samuel went to grab another coffee and then returned to his desk, watching as the lines of code flashed across the screen, a hypnotic representation of the model's complex algorithms.

The intersection of technology and ancient history had always fascinated him, and Samuel was grateful to live at this moment in time where AI tools amplified human ability, allowing him to see patterns and connections that might have taken years to discern in the past.

For generations, archaeology had been about painstaking manual labour, endless hours spent digging, cataloguing, and theorising. Samuel enjoyed that part of the process — the physical connection to the earth and the artefacts, the feeling of holding history in his hands — but artificial intelligence had transformed his field into something even greater.

He found the AI tools augmented his skills and amplified his curiosity. He could feed his model fragments — images, patterns, data points, scans — and it would work tirelessly to untangle complexity, making associations and offering theories he could expand based on his knowledge.

The machine offered insights, but it could never fathom true meaning or answer the human questions that the site raised. Why was the henge built? Was it an open burial for a revered creature or a sacrificial offering to the gods? There were so many questions that perhaps he might discover answers to in the symbols.

Samuel leaned forward and tapped a few keys to refine the model's parameters. He watched the machine adjust and adapt, recalculating possibilities in real time, then leaned back in his chair and sipped his coffee as the intricate lines of the model evolved, layer by layer, on the screen.

*   *   *

The soft chime of his computer pulled Samuel back to consciousness. He must have dropped off to sleep at some point. It was almost 4:00 a.m. and Evelyn and the team would be back in an hour or so. He didn't have much time left.

His screen showed the next set of results from the model's analysis, and he grabbed another coffee before evaluating them.

It had found recurring patterns that seemed to describe a catastrophic event. Symbols of water, sky, and land arranged in configurations that suggested upheaval and destruction.

"A flood myth," Samuel whispered, his mind racing with the implications. Nearly every culture on Earth had stories of great floods, of worlds drowned and remade.

He dug deeper into the analysis, cross-referencing the symbols with known flood myths from cultures around the world.

The parallels were striking, but there were elements here that didn't fit any known mythology. It described not just a flood, but a cycle of floods. Catastrophic inundations that came at regular intervals.

As he considered the implications, Samuel spun in his chair and looked over at the tank across the lab.

The mermaid floated in the preservation tank, her form both familiar and strange. Had the Neolithic tribe created this hybrid creature as an offering to the sea — a desperate attempt to keep the floods at bay?

Or if such creatures lived alongside humanity, might the sacrifice have been a warning or a threat from the Neolithic people to those of the sea?

"We will destroy those who threaten us," he murmured, imagining the message carried across millennia.

Samuel turned back to his screen, forcing himself to focus on the data. It was the only way he would find answers.

There was something in the next section of symbols, a pattern that the model suggested might be an invocation of some kind, linked to a blood offering.

He frowned and tapped away at his keyboard. Perhaps bringing in another comparison culture would help.

He settled on the Vinča culture, an early Neolithic society that flourished in south-eastern Europe. They developed a complex system of symbols that some researchers believed to be one of the earliest forms of writing.

Samuel input the parameters, instructing the model to compare the Seahenge symbols with Vinča script.

As the program began its analysis, he leaned back in his chair, rubbing his tired eyes. The faint hum of the computers and the gentle lapping of water in the preservation tank broke the silence of the lab.

His screen shifted once more as the model found patterns and similarities, particularly those associated with water and celestial bodies, hinting at sacrifice and appeasement of a greater power.

Samuel leaned in closer.

The central stump seemed to be the key, as the model highlighted it as a focal point.

There was also a recurring sequence that could be interpreted as a kind of countdown to the end of a cycle. But what cycle? The end of a lunar phase? A tidal pattern?

The sound of car engines and slamming doors came from outside. Soon the chatter of the arriving workers filled the kitchen area downstairs as the team grabbed coffee and went over plans for the final retrieval.

Evelyn strode into Samuel's office, her eyes bright with excitement despite the early hour. "Morning. Find anything interesting?"

He gestured to his screens. "Lots to unpack from the analysis. There's something important about that central stump, but I can't quite piece it together yet."

Evelyn leaned in and scanned the complex patterns on the screen. "Looks fascinating. This is going to take us years to process and publish. Perhaps the stump has symbols on it as well. You can check them once we get it back here. If the weather holds long enough, we'll get it out before high tide."

A gust of wind rattled the lab windows.

Samuel looked out into the dawn light to see dark clouds gathering on the horizon over the sea, the promise of the storm returning with full force. The ancient civilisations he had studied all paid attention to signs and portents in nature, and although the modern world of science and technology was sceptical about such things, Samuel couldn't help but wonder if sometimes the omens were right.

He looked up at Evelyn. "Be careful out there. We don't know what we're dealing with."

She put a hand on his shoulder and smiled. "You do your job, I'll do mine. We have all the right equipment and safety procedures in place for such a heavy object. We've recovered ancient ships before, so I'm sure we can manage a tree stump."

He nodded. "Of course. See you later then, hopefully with the last piece of this puzzle."

Evelyn headed back down, and within minutes the entire team was gone, leaving Samuel in the quiet. There was nothing he could say to stop them. His fears were as yet unfounded, but he couldn't ignore the growing dread that rose within, and it drove him on.

His fingers flew over the keyboard, inputting new parameters, cross-referencing data sets. The model continued refining its analysis, churning through vast amounts of data as patterns emerged, dissolved, and reformed in new configurations. Samuel glanced between the screens, his mind racing to keep up.

A low rumble of thunder sounded in the distance, and the lab lights flickered.

Samuel glanced up, momentarily distracted, and as he looked back at the screen, he noticed something new.

The model had isolated a sequence of symbols that suggested a barrier of some kind, a wall that held back the flood.

The timbers had been arranged in a circle, so they touched each other, forming a barricade. Perhaps that's what it referred to?

But the scale of the language was more like the great epic of Gilgamesh, a flood that would destroy the known world, not just a tiny corner of an English county.

As the wind howled outside, and the rain hammered down on the roof, Samuel worked on.

He was so close. He just needed more time.

CHAPTER 4

DOWN AT THE BEACH, Evelyn braced herself against the stinging sand and salt whirling in amongst the driving rain. The wind whipped across the towering waves that crashed only metres from the last remaining piece of Seahenge.

The central stump stood defiant against the elements, its gnarled roots reaching up towards the dark clouds. The surrounding timbers that had protected it for millennia were all back at the lab now and they had to get this final piece out before the tide swallowed it once more.

As a gust of wind took her breath away, Evelyn wondered whether it would be better to wait and try again tomorrow. Logic said that the stump would re-emerge once more as the tide went out again in its ever-repeating cycle, but she had a sense they didn't have much time. It was as if the sea wanted to reclaim what had lain in its embrace for so long.

The snap of canvas rang through the air.

Evelyn spun around. "Secure that line!" she shouted over the howling wind.

One of her team members grabbed the flying end of a long belt, used to secure the cargo. Several others went to help and together, they regained control, their years of practiced efficiency evident even in the difficult conditions.

The huge truck backed once more down the beach, sinking a little into the compacted sand, then swung its crane above the tree stump. The team carefully wrapped the wood above the sand-line, boxing in the upper roots to protect them, and packing the deepening wound in the core with cloth to strengthen it.

Finally, the team moved back, waiting for the 'go' signal.

Evelyn's heart beat faster in her chest as she walked forward for one last check. They needed to do as much as possible to protect the ancient timber as once they started to lift, the whole thing could disintegrate — and that would be on her.

She circled the stump, checking that the protective padding and straps were firm enough. Even through her gloves, she could feel the contours of the ancient wood, ridges and whorls shaped by millennia under the peat, beneath the sea. Could these symbols unlock the meaning of the site?

A cacophony of piercing cries split the air.

A flock of gulls wheeled overhead, fighting against the wind to stay above the tree stump, their gaze fixed on the scene below. They were no doubt waiting to see what creatures might emerge from under the stump once it was removed, but Evelyn couldn't help feeling that these guardians of the sea called a warning of some kind.

As she looked up at them, her fingers brushed against one of the upturned roots. A chill spiked the hairs on the back of her neck.

Something was watching.

She turned to look out to sea, her breath catching in her throat as she saw immense dark shadows rising from the deep, circling closer to shore.

"Evelyn, are you alright?"

The voice of one of her team broke through the darker thoughts and Evelyn jerked her hand away from the root. The shadows in the water were just reflections of the storm clouds or silt boiled up by the churning of the sea.

She stepped away from the stump. "Yes, I think we're ready to start. Slowly now. Everyone ready?"

A chorus of affirmatives sounded from her team as they moved into position.

Evelyn stepped back, her gaze never leaving the stump as the crane's winch engine roared to life.

The straps around the stump drew taut, creaking under the strain.

For a moment, nothing happened.

Then, with agonising slowness, the ancient wood began to shift.

"Easy does it," Evelyn murmured. "Nice and slow."

The stump rose inch by inch, fighting against the suction of the sand and peat that had held it for millennia.

The tension in the straps hummed, vibrating with the weight of the ancient timber and the force of the sea still tugging at its foundation. The wood creaked and popped, echoing like the splintering of old bones, the sound sharp beneath the steady patter of rain on sand.

As it lifted, Evelyn crouched to look into a gap beneath the branches of the tree which held it in the peat. Something glinted down there.

"Hold!" she shouted.

The crane operator immediately halted the lift.

She approached the partially raised stump, knelt in the sand, and shone her torch into the gap.

The light glinted off a knife, its blade dark with age. The handle was intricately carved with images of waves and sea life, along with strange, tentacled creatures alongside merfolk. Its placement suggested ritual use. Perhaps it was even the blade that killed the creature from the roots above.

A massive wave crashed on the sand, sending a pool of icy water into the depression holding the knife, before drawing back to the deep.

There was no time to waste.

Evelyn quickly took a few photos of the knife in situ with her phone and readied herself to take more as the stump rose.

She took a step back and waved at the truck driver. "Resume the lift!"

As the stump rose inch by inch, and the last of the branches pulled out of the peat, a flash of forked lightning split the air, followed immediately by a deep rumble of thunder.

The storm was upon them.

CHAPTER 5

SAMUEL WAS ALMOST DELIRIOUS now with lack of sleep and too much caffeine, but he could sense he was close, so close, to cracking the code.

He needed a new perspective and perhaps there were some things that weren't in the language corpus.

Samuel headed out of the lab and down into the library, a place he rarely visited since he found most of his reference material online now.

The dusty shelves of the library's archaeology section held volumes that had never been digitised, their spines cracked and yellowed with age. Samuel pulled down several books on ancient scripts and underwater archaeology, spreading them across a worn oak table beneath flickering fluorescent lights.

He examined diagrams of cuneiform tablets from Mesopotamia and fragments of Linear A from Minoan Crete, but these were all known to his model. Then he found a beautifully hand-illustrated book on submerged cities. While photographs were included in his model, illustrations were considered to be potentially misleading as a source.

The book detailed ruins found beneath the waves:

the temples of Mahabalipuram off the coast of India, drowned by rising seas six thousand years ago; the fractured columns of Thonis-Heracleion in Egypt's Abu Qir Bay, swallowed by the Mediterranean; and most intriguingly, the massive stone formations of Yonaguni, thought to be ten thousand years old off Japan.

Samuel quickly snapped pictures of the relevant pages and diagrams with his phone, his mind already racing ahead to how the new data might change the model. It could find patterns across things that didn't seem logical for humans, connections that spanned millennia and continents, and he could only hope this was the key.

Back at his desk, he uploaded the photos and clicked to re-run the analysis.

He watched as the status bar slowly inched towards completion.

Suddenly, the model shifted.

The screen flickered, and a new translation emerged, based not just on the individual markings, but on the entire pattern of the Seahenge site itself.

Samuel's heart raced as he read the output.

The barrier around the central stump wasn't just a protective shield for the site — it was something far more significant.

The upturned tree was a ritual focal point, a nexus empowered by ancient blood and salt magic. It was a seal, sanctified with the sacrifice of a daughter of the sea.

He sat back, his mind reeling.

A seal.

The word echoed in his head as he considered the implications. A seal was placed over something to keep it secure, to keep a bottle stoppered, to prevent something from being released. But what could be so terrible that it required such elaborate containment?

He frowned as the model beeped again, returning a new translation of the key text: "What has been drowned will be drowned again."

Before he could even process the disturbing words, the image of the site on his screen transformed.

A star chart materialised, superimposing itself over the placement of the timber circle, with an explanation of a timeline next to it.

But it wasn't the constellation of the Neolithic sky. It was the celestial configuration of the present day.

Samuel's hand trembled as he reached for his phone, frantically dialling Evelyn.

He had to stop her. He had to prevent the removal of the stump. Whatever secrets Seahenge held, it was far more than just a historical artefact.

They needed more time — time to decipher, to understand, and to prepare for whatever terrible truth lay buried beneath the sand.

The phone rang on, but Evelyn didn't pick up.

A blinding flash of lightning split the sky outside, followed immediately by a deafening crack of thunder that shook the building to its foundations. The lights overhead flickered once, twice, and then plunged the lab into darkness.

Samuel sat paralysed with indecision. Was he overreacting? Could his model be flawed, leading him down a path of baseless paranoia? How could something so ancient, buried for millennia, suddenly pose a threat in modern times?

Doubt gnawed at the edges of his mind. Had he fed too many conspiracy theories into the model?

The emergency lights sputtered to life, casting an eerie, blood-red glow across the lab.

Samuel looked over at the preservation tank on the far side of the room. The mermaid was impossible, and yet, here she was. The truth of her existence sparked a deep fear in him. Something made from fragments of humanity's collective unconscious, passed down through the genetic line.

This was real.

He had to get to the beach. He had to stop Evelyn before it was too late.

Samuel scrambled for the door, bumping into workstations and scattering papers in his haste.

He burst out of the lab and into the raging storm. Rain lashed his face and gusts of wind threatened to knock him off his feet.

Lightning illuminated the parking lot in stuttering flashes as Samuel hurried to his car, fumbling with the keys as another crash of thunder growled overhead. The engine roared to life, and he sped out of the car park, tires skidding on the rain-slicked road.

It wasn't far to the beach, but it seemed as if the storm conspired to stop him making headway. He drove into the wind, the car slowing, as trees by the side of the road bent double in the gale.

Samuel hunched forward, straining to see through the veil of water. He could hardly make out anything, the wipers useless against the deluge.

As he navigated a treacherous bend, the car hydroplaned, sliding sideways with sickening momentum. He gripped the steering wheel, fighting to regain control.

As the tires found purchase once more, a branch blew from a tree, smashing into the windscreen.

Samuel braked, panting with shock, but the wind rolled it off the car and there was only a little damage.

He drove on, rounding the last corner to the car park overlooking the beach, and parked close to the edge.

As he fought against the howling wind, Samuel pushed open the door and staggered to the edge of the embankment. Rain stung his eyes, blurring his vision as he desperately searched the scene below.

Through the curtain of rain, illuminated by work lights that cut through the gloom, he could see the crane was moving. Its massive arm swung ponderously through the air, bearing aloft its ancient burden — the central tree stump of Seahenge, finally wrenched free.

He was too late. The seal was broken.

CHAPTER 6

EVELYN WATCHED THE STUMP rise from the sand, willing it to stay in one piece. The ancient wood creaked and groaned as the crane lifted the last piece of Seahenge and winched it towards the back of the preservation truck.

Once the stump was clear of the sand, Evelyn darted forward and, using her beanie hat as make-shift protection, she grabbed the handle of the knife.

As she lifted it away from its resting place, water rushed from the holes left by the stump. It was dark and thick with peat, surging up as if an underground reservoir had been breached.

The crack in the sand that had appeared yesterday suddenly widened with alarming speed, opening a deep fissure that rapidly filled with dark water.

Evelyn stumbled away, clutching the knife to her chest. "Get back, everyone!"

A deafening shriek filled the air as the gulls circled overhead, then darted away inland, their wings beating frantically against the howling wind as if they fled an encroaching terror.

Evelyn turned towards the sea, her breath catching in her throat.

The waves were retreating, pulling back farther than she'd ever seen. Flopping fish and stranded crustaceans covered the exposed seafloor, helpless as the water abandoned them.

As the sea drew back, it piled upon itself, building into a wall of water that towered over the beach, higher and higher with every second.

"Impossible," Evelyn whispered, her mind reeling. "A tsunami? Here?"

But this was no ordinary wave.

The shadows within shifted into dark, writhing forms that seemed too vast, too alien to be any sea life she recognised.

As much as her scientist brain refused to think it true, they had awoken something ancient with the desecration of Seahenge and the removal of its sacred dead.

"Get off the beach!" Evelyn turned to her team and shouted, her voice barely audible over the roar of the wind. "Now! We have to get to higher ground!"

Her team scrambled up the beach, abandoning equipment and racing for their cars.

But even as they ran, Evelyn knew they couldn't possibly get as far away as they needed to in time.

As the sea continued to draw back, exposing more and more of the seafloor, she understood the true scale of what was coming.

This wasn't just a threat to their stretch of beach. This was a flood that would swallow the entire Fens, a vast swathe of low-lying land that had once belonged to the sea. Land that humans, in their hubris, had drained and built upon over centuries.

Land that was about to be drowned once more.

The Seahenge timbers, the remains of the mermaid — all would be swallowed by the sea, along with countless other lives and homes.

Even if they could sound an evacuation now, it would be too late.

As Evelyn ran up the embankment towards the car park, she saw Samuel, his expression etched with horror.

She sprinted towards him, her feet slipping in the wet sand as she struggled against the wind.

"I tried to get here in time to stop you," Samuel shouted as she drew close, his words nearly lost in the howling gale. "I'm so sorry."

"It doesn't matter now. Let's get to higher ground." Evelyn jumped in the back of his car as three others crammed into the vehicle.

Samuel gunned the engine.

As they sped away from the beach, Evelyn twisted in her seat to look out the rear window.

The wall of water grew ever higher as it pulled back. When it rushed in once more, it would be a tsunami of mythic proportions. A flood of future legend.

Vast, dark shapes moved in its depths with tentacles as thick as the ancient oak spars of Seahenge. They writhed and reached for the shore, as if trying to grasp the land the wave sought to reclaim.

Images from ancient myth flashed through Evelyn's mind — the Kraken of Norse legend, the multi-headed Hydra of Greek tales, the biblical Leviathan.

Among these larger forms, she glimpsed smaller humanoid figures with powerful tails instead of legs. Merfolk, not the beautiful ones of fairy tale, but primal creatures with teeth and claws to rip apart their prey.

"What have we done?" Evelyn breathed, her voice barely a whisper.

As the car sped away from the beach, heading for higher ground, Samuel hit a wide puddle and skidded on the road. The water was deep, and the car sputtered and died as the engine flooded.

He cursed, frantically trying to restart it, but Evelyn knew it was useless. They had gone as far as they could.

The small group abandoned the vehicle and ran for a nearby hill, trying to climb higher, seeking refuge from the flood that would surely come.

They reached the top of the hill quickly. It was too small to be of any protection, and they turned together to watch as the wall of water pulled back even further. It was gigantic and Evelyn felt a sense of awe to see its power in the moments before it was unleashed.

She clutched the sacred knife to her chest, unwilling to let it go, a reminder of the hubris that had led them to this moment. Not just her own choice to desecrate the ancient site, but the decisions of generations before her who drained this fenland, thinking they could live upon land stolen from the sea.

"What was drowned will be drowned again," Samuel murmured beside her.

Far out across the sands, the sea seemed to gather itself, darkening as it heaved upward, swelling into something unnatural.

There was no rolling crest, no gentle rise.

This was a wall of water — solid, impenetrable, growing taller with each second until it was a black mass that blotted out the horizon, sucking the light from the sky.

The roar that followed was delayed, like thunder after lightning, a deep, primal sound that reverberated through the air, growing louder as the wave rushed forward.

A sheer, towering face of water surging toward the land with terrifying, unstoppable force.

Evelyn watched it come with a strange calm. The world they knew was ending, and what would emerge from this second great flood, she couldn't begin to imagine.

The last thing she saw before the waters swept over her was a massive shadow, its tentacles like the roots of the Seahenge tree, reaching once more for the sky.

AUTHOR'S NOTE

While my story and characters are fiction, Seahenge itself is real.

In 2022, I went to an exhibition at the British Museum on The World of Stonehenge, where some of the ancient timbers of Seahenge were on display. As I stood in front of them and imagined what the central upturned trunk of the tree looked like with a sacrifice on top of it, I knew I would write a story about it someday.

In September 2024, I visited Ely Cathedral, known as the Ship of the Fens. It once stood on an island amongst the flat flooded plains of Norfolk, which have been repeatedly drained over centuries so people could live on dry land.

You can see my pictures of Ely Cathedral here: www.booksandtravel.page/ely-cathedral

It rained while I was there and I began to think about the circle of time and how, with climate change and sea levels rising, this area would once more belong to the sea. If you look at potential maps of how the UK might look in 2030 to 2050, that area is almost always flooded.

Seahenge is also known as Holme I and is a

prehistoric timber circle originally located near Holme-next-the-Sea in Norfolk, England. It dates to the Early Bronze Age, around 2049 BC, and consists of fifty-five oak posts arranged in a circle over six meters in diameter. A large, upturned tree stump at its centre with its roots in the air formed a platform.

While the exact nature of the circle is unknown, some propose it could have been used for sky burial, where a corpse is placed in the centre, surrounded by a wall of timbers to protect it. The elements and carrion birds slowly take the remains back into the circle of nature. I've written about such practices in *Destroyer of Worlds* and there is still a Zoroastrian Tower of Silence in Mumbai.

The Seahenge site was discovered in 1998 when the sands shifted to reveal the staves hidden under layers of peat, which preserved the wood in the salt marsh. The timbers and stump were removed, treated for preservation, and now stand on display at Lynn Museum in King's Lynn, Norfolk.

Peat can preserve human remains as evidenced by Lindow Man, but of course, there was no body found at Seahenge, mermaid or otherwise.

Artificial intelligence (AI) models are already being used in archaeology, with no doubt more advances to come.

A paper in *Nature* in 2023 outlined the way human–AI collaboration might work for archaeological site detection with fine-tuned models overlaid on satellite or aerial imagery. An article on Historica.org lists the different ways that AI is already used, from detecting hidden sites in scans to translating ancient languages and analysing historical texts.

Related links and Bibliography

Sunken Lands: A Journey Through Flooded Kingdoms and Lost Worlds — Gareth E. Rees

Seahenge: A Quest for Life and Death in Bronze Age Britain — Francis Pryor

My photos from a trip to Ely Cathedral — www.booksandtravel.page/ely-cathedral

British Museum World of Stonehenge exhibition — www.britishmuseum.org/exhibitions/world-stonehenge

Seahenge at Lynn Museum, Norfolk — www.lynnmuseum.norfolk.gov.uk/article/30498/Seahenge-gallery-at-Lynn-Museum

"Lindow Man: Gruesome discovery who became 'international celebrity.'" BBC News, 3 August

2014. Accessed 10 October 2024 —
www.bbc.co.uk/news/uk-england-28589151

Potential flood maps with predictions of land that
might be flooded, which includes Norfolk —
https://coastal.climatecentral.org/map/

"A human–AI collaboration workflow for archaeological sites detection," *Nature*, 29 May 2023 —
www.nature.com/articles/s41598-023-36015-5

"The Latest AI Innovations in Archaeology," His-
torica, 15 August 2024, accessed 16 October 2024
— https://www.historica.org/blog/the-latest-ai-
innovations-in-archaeology

ACKNOWLEDGEMENTS

Thanks to Mark Leslie Lefebvre for encouraging me to write short stories and commissioning my first short story more than a decade ago.

Thanks to my editor, Kristen Tate at The Blue Garret, and my cover designer, Jane Dixon Smith at JD Smith Design.

MORE BOOKS BY J.F. PENN

ARKANE Action-Adventure Thrillers

Stone of Fire #1
Crypt of Bone #2
Ark of Blood #3
One Day in Budapest #4
Day of the Vikings #5
Gates of Hell #6
One Day in New York #7
Destroyer of Worlds #8
End of Days #9
Valley of Dry Bones #10
Tree of Life #11
Tomb of Relics #12
[Stand-alone ARKANE story — Soldiers of God]
Spear of Destiny #13

Brooke and Daniel Psychological/Crime Thrillers

Desecration #1
Delirium #2
Deviance #3

Mapwalker Dark Fantasy Adventures

Map of Shadows #1
Map of Plagues #2
Map of the Impossible #3

Horror

Catacomb
Risen Gods
Blood Vintage

Short Stories

A Thousand Fiendish Angels
The Dark Queen
A Midwinter Sacrifice
Blood, Sweat, and Flame
With a Demon's Eye
Beneath the Zoo
De-extinction of the Nephilim

Travel Memoir

Pilgrimage:
Lessons Learned from Solo Walking Three
Ancient Ways

More books coming soon …

You can sign up to be notified of new releases, giveaways and pre-release specials - plus, get a free ebook!

WWW.JFPENN.COM/FREE

If you loved the book and have a moment to spare, I would really appreciate a short review on the page where you bought the book.

Your help in spreading the word is gratefully appreciated and reviews make a huge difference to helping new readers find the series. Thank you!

ABOUT J.F. PENN

J.F. Penn is the Award-winning, New York Times and USA Today bestselling author of thrillers, dark fantasy, crime, horror, short stories, and travel memoir.

Jo lives in Bath, England and enjoys a nice G&T.

You can find my J.F. Penn Reading Order at:
www.jfpenn.com/readingorder

Buy books directly from me:

www.JFPennBooks.com

* * *

Sign up for your free thriller, Day of the Vikings, and receive updates from behind the scenes, research, and giveaways at:

WWW.JFPENN.COM/FREE

* * *

Connect with Jo:
www.JFPenn.com
Instagram @jfpennauthor
Facebook @jfpennauthor
X @thecreativepenn
www.BooksAndTravel.page

* * *

Love books and travel?

Check out my Books and Travel Podcast on your favorite podcast app, or find the backlist at:

www.BooksAndTravel.page/listen

For writers:

Joanna's site, www.TheCreativePenn.com empowers authors with the knowledge they need to choose their creative future. Books by Joanna Penn, as well as her award-winning show, *The Creative Penn Podcast*, provide information and inspiration on writing craft and creative business.